Meet Me
On The Ice

Melanie Davies

Meet Me On The Ice

MELANIE DAVIES

For those who continue to heal and find strength in themselves.

CHAPTER 1
Kimberly

*I*t will get easier hunny, trust me, this pain won't last forever. My mother's voice echoed through my mind as I held a photograph of my wedding day, our wedding day. Luke beamed with glee, wearing the brightest and widest smile I had ever seen, and it was all for me, as we stood under the altar in our families church. The church he begged me to marry him in and now, I couldn't even step foot in.

I went through and put the last of his things away, and all the grief and pain of his death had been brought back to the forefront. I tried to hold myself together, to not cry, but tears still escaped. Placing the photograph back into our wedding album and sticking it gently in a box, his favorite winter scarf caught my eye and as I held it up, his scent, his aftershave, came flooding into my senses.

He always smelt of a warm fire on a winter's night. We only had a short marriage before God stepped in and took him from me, just shy of our fourth wedding anniversary. I thought we'd beaten the odds, he wasn't going to be a part of the statistics and it wasn't even the dreaded 'C' that got him in the end, it was the blood clot they missed in his heart.

I was grateful in some ways he went quick, asleep on the operating table and not awake in pain. We even had a lovely day together the day before his operation, which I will never forget. Did I regret not telling him I loved him that night? Did I even say it that day? I couldn't remember, it had been a year since and only now had I found some strength to put his things away and head back to work. I need to find who I was without him. *Without him.*

Putting everything back into the box, I taped it shut and as much as it pained me, I took it down to the garage. The box was placed on one of the shelves, along with the other keepsakes. I had already donated his clothes and books to people in need, but I couldn't fully part with everything.

Looking at my watch, I noticed it was just past eight in the morning. It was my first day back at work. I had to leave soon if I am to prove to everyone I am doing alright, perfectly fine, even if deep down I'm not. And yet, a brave mask went on as I knew the excuse of 'my husband died' was wearing thin.

"Be good, Daisy, I won't be long."

Bending down to touch noses with my beautiful fluffy companion, I gave her head a rub. I grabbed my keys, my ice-skates and bag, before I headed out the door. I was to coach some new recruits, prepare them for the figure skating regionals and hopefully go onto nationals.

Getting back into the rhythm of work was going to take some getting used to and as much as I wanted to stay home and lie in bed, in my grief, I had young teenagers to train. A group of adolescents who had passed their child examinations and were now making their way up the ranks.

I had stopped listening to music since Luke's death, but I knew as soon as I entered the ice rink there would be music blasting from the speakers and I just had to ignore it. He was such a big music lover, every morning he had to have the radio playing, or some playlist he had conjured up the night before, but now it just brought me heartache. Which was a little silly, as he had always said, music can help with all sorts of emotions.

The rink was quiet this morning, aside from the Zamboni making its way across the ice and the staff bustling about. They were cleaning up the spectator chairs from the night before as well as opening the café and ice skate rental stall. I had to head to Rachel's office once I arrived, to get a briefing of any changes that had happened while I was on leave, and I dreaded the questions I knew that were going to be fired at me.

Knocking on her door before opening it, I saw she was already in a meeting with someone but before I could escape, she spotted me.

"Oh, Kimberly, lovely to see you, please, come in."

"I don't mind waiting outside."

"That's alright, we were just finishing up. This is Samuel, he's on leave with his eh - work and has offered to coach the new children's ice hockey team."

He stood up and I realized I hadn't noticed how much his broad shoulders filled the small office chair. I wouldn't have guessed that he was as tall as he appeared to be, standing at least six foot three. God like, was all I could think looking at his sunkissed brown skin, unkempt brown hair and green eyes that were set upon me.

Samuel Jones, captain of the Vancouver Devils, the boy who had stolen my heart back in high school was now standing in front of me after nearly ten years of only seeing him on television screens and news articles.

"It's lovely to see you again, Kimmy."

My heart stopped in my chest as I felt a bead of sweat run down my back. It felt like time hadn't moved since junior high, he hadn't changed a bit, other than grown more into himself and definitely more handsome than when he was a pimple-nosed teen.

"Ah, you guys know each other?" Rachel stepped in.

"Yeah, me and Kim go way back!" Exclaimed Samuel with a smile on his face.

"We, eh, we went to junior high together, and we had a few classes together, I think."

A small lie, but Rachel didn't need to know our full history and I was hoping Samuel caught my drift. I didn't like sharing all my business with my boss, only the things she needed to know, and these things had happened in the past, way deep in the past.

"Lovely, well Sam, Kimberly is our figure skating coach, so I'm sure you will be seeing plenty of each other during lessons. Kim starts training our newest team today, after taking a long leave of absence."

"Yeah, I heard about your husband, I'm sorry for your loss."

"Thank you."

How did he hear about that? He was off being some super famous ice hockey player. Perhaps he was being kept in the loop by his parents; they still lived in the same house on Wicker Street, after all. There was an awkward silence that settled in the air before Samuel realized it was time for him to take his leave - in order for Rachel and me to get on with our own meeting.

"Well, it was nice seeing you Kim, and Rachel, thanks for this. After my injury, my manager advised me to get some rest, so I will be missing out on this winter season and as this place gave birth to my career, it's only fair I offer to help others."

He smiled sweetly to me as he passed by and shut the door behind himself, and I felt my heart slow down to a regular pace at last. Seeing his face was the last thing I needed, especially today while I had to keep myself composed.

I opted to stay standing while Rachel and I discussed the new staff schedule, the training calendar as well as the events that would be taking place this season. With Christmas just around the corner, a mere three months away, we needed to get our asses in gear and get my team up to date.

"ALRIGHT, girls, thank you for showing up today - That makes this todays class at least off to a good start."

Arms crossed and at the ready, my new trainees all look as nervous as I felt inside, eagerly awaiting my orders, but I'm not as tough as the younger childrens' coach. No, I was worse.

"Now, I have three rules as your new coach. One, I don't like nasty sneaky bitches, if you want to destroy another girl's ice career, you have to go through me first."

I paused looking at each of them, all prim and proper, with tough parents who would give them everything they ever asked for. Whereas I came from two hard working parents, who could barely afford to put the heating on when it got cold. I learned how to skate on the frozen lake outside of our house. It wasn't until my moms accident at work, did things start looking up for us when she had the payout.

"Second rule, not everyone has the advantages you are blessed with. Some aren't able to pay for ice skating lessons from the time they can walk, some may work a part-time job to pay for their classes and wear rented or gifted skates. Don't judge."

One of the girls rolled her eyes and smiled snarkily. It

made my blood boil as I marked her card there and then. She was going to either be the one who gave me trouble or was the secretly insecure one who would try to ruin someone else's confidence.

"Thirdly, we are a team first and foremost, we take care of our own. Yes, you may compete against each other, but soon you will get to know each other and become a family. Protect your own. Now, give me ten laps around the rink for a warmup. Go!"

Watching them skate off, I headed to the rink gate to get my bag. I needed to grab a mint and a couple deep breaths. Already my stomach was cramping from the stress and tears I held tightly inwards, the stress piling on my shoulders. Rolling them then cracking my neck, the girls went past me a few times before I noticed Samuel was sitting a few rows back watching.

"It's nice to see you here," he said, as he caught me watching him. "It's nice to be back here."

I didn't respond, just smiled, then looked back at the girls unsure of what number lap they were on.

"They're on lap six," he said as he appeared next to me, frightening the life out of me.

"Jesus! Don't sneak up on people like that!" I shouted, stepping away from him.

"Ha ha. Sorry, Kimmy."

"Kimberly," I corrected him.

"Sorry, Kimberly." That smile again, but I rolled my eyes in reply instead of falling for it.

"Why are you really here, Sam? It can't actually be to teach kids ice-hockey. You were never the charitable kind."

He put his hands in his pockets and lowered his eyes a little, kicking the floor beneath him. Clearly ready to tell a lie, his tells were still the same as they were when we were teenagers. Then he looked at me, and he appeared to struggle for a moment before answering, sounding surprisingly sincere.

"My manager, he benched me, I was eh – getting aggressive with some of my teammates, and yeah…"

"Ahh, so this is a publicity stunt then, you're hoping the media catches wind of this and makes you out to be this perfect guy who helps disadvantaged kids learn how to play an amazing sport. Pretend all you want, Sam, all of us in this place know who you really are."

I had already caught onto his game, he had always been the aggressive type of guy, but never violent, he just hated backing down. I heard about his several bar fights when he left the town as well as the many arguments he'd had with his team. I had always been surprised he had done as well as he did, but then again he had a full scholarship to Ohio State University and therefore a free ride to do as he pleased, as long as he played well and got those goals.

"It's not like that Kimberly – I'm not like that anymore."

"Yeah, yeah, I will believe it when I see it, now if you will excuse me, I have a class to teach."

Getting back on the ice, I started to teach the girls the basics of advanced ice-skating, the way to hold yourself safely, to look after your partner. Near the end of their introduction lesson, I tasked them with picking a song and coming up with a small two-minute routine to show me what they could do. Which, to my surprise, they were all very excited to do.

By the time I was leaving, school was out, and public skating had begun. I couldn't wait to be home to wallow in grief with Daisy at my side cuddling under a blanket while we watched Hallmark Christmas movies. But sadly, by the time I picked up my phone and headed to the car - Crystal, was calling.

My out of this world gorgeous curvy bestie, who owned one of the best cafes in the entire city of Vancouver. She was ordering me around, demanding I come in for a free lunch and a catch up. I had been avoiding her pretty much for weeks. I did feel bad about it, after all she just wanted to be there for me and yet, I felt suffocated and needed space from everyone.

"Alright – let me head home and grab Daisy and I will be with you in twenty, but no drinks, only coffee."

"Don't be long missy! We miss you here."

Throwing my phone back in my bag and heading home, I quickly changed into a pair of jeans, a fall themed sweatshirt, and threw on my riding boots and a warm coat. Although the leaves are only now starting to change, I knew it was going to get colder by the evening and warmth was a must.

Daisy seemed very happy to be going out as my poor girly had been stuck indoors all afternoon, well at least since the dog walker put her back in. I hated not being home with her all day, but I knew we both needed a little space from each other.

Driving through town was such a lovely experience especially since everyone had started to decorate their homes and shop windows with winter decorations. Many still had their fall decorations up, but it still worked. The town was filled with beautiful shades of blues, oranges, whites, yellows, and obviously, Christmas colors.

During my years away at Boston University, I always missed home. I missed the closeness of everyone knowing one another, that family feeling you had from your neighbors being friendly or when an event went on, you knew it was going to be great fun as everyone would pull together and make it awesome.

Finally, I parked outside *The Wooden Spoon*, Crystal's

swanky café that she had to fight to get. The thousands of outdoor lights she had decorated the rooftop and windows with were almost blinding people as they passed and I had to laugh, she always did things a little extra.

"KIM!" She shouted at me from behind the counter as I opened the front door. "DAISY!" And of course, she appeared to be happier to see the dog than me. "Come here my beautiful, fluffy girly."

Dressed in what could only be described as eccentric and colorful, Crystal came down to Daisy's level and gave her the biggest hug a dog could get before finally coming over to give me one.

"It's so wonderful to see you, girly, are you ok? How was your first day back?"

"First, coffee then questions. Also, when did you cut your hair?"

Crystal used to have beautiful long brown hair, now she had dyed her hair black, and it was sitting just below her ears, in a cute little bob. She spun around and flashed a beautiful smile my way, her gypsy style forest green dress spun around her ankles along with her waterfall sleeved blouse. She was channeling her inner Stevie Nick's.

"What'd you think? I was feeling my gothic, witchy self."

"I love it and it definitely fits in with your witchy vibes."

Taking my usual seat near the left-hand window, Daisy settled on the dog bed that was provided just for her. *The Wooden Spoon* was, of course, a dog friendly café. However, it was very rare anyone actually brought their dogs in, except for myself and Mrs. Holly, the town's grandma.

Crystal was soon sitting opposite me with a tray of coffee and cake. The café was quiet aside from Gerald, the regular who always sat on the comfortable sofas reading a book. He had been coming here since the day Crystal opened the doors.

I had mentioned to her that he clearly fancied her, but nope, Crystal wouldn't have any of it.

"Say, have you had your cards read, you know, since..."

"No, and I don't plan to."

"Alright, still a sore subject I see, sorry." She sipped her coffee and kept her eyes from me, smiling. "Did you hear who's back in town?"

The best thing about running a café - especially the only one that sold the best Victorian Chocolate Sponge Cake in the whole city - was you got to hear all sorts of gossip and yet, I was pretty sure I knew this piece before Crystal had even heard it.

"Samuel Jones is back in town," I cut her off.

"How the hell did you know that already!" She asked me, almost slamming her cup down.

"Wouldn't you like to know," I winked jokingly. "Nah, actually, he was at the rink this morning, apparently he's offered to train the kids ice-hockey team for the winter season."

"Well, that's not suspicious, wonder what that's code for."

"Not code for anything he says. Rachel mentioned he will be gone by the time January rolls around, so I wouldn't pay too much attention."

"But Kim, he was like your first love, love of your life kind of thing."

"No, Luke was the love of my life. Sam was a mistake and something I did during my teens."

We may have had a history, a very intense passionate history together, but that was all it was. History. We were a junior figure skater and a senior ice-hockey player, but of course we had ended up together, secretly. No one really knew other than Crystal. For the most part of it, Sam had ignored me in the halls of school, but yet kissed me in the locker room away from everyone. He had been ashamed of me, a girl from the poorer part of town, and he was the son of a coach at the time. The coach that had sent many hockey players off on their amazing careers.

We would never have worked and when he had left for college, I went into senior year and that was it. Heck he invited me to prom, then didn't show up and that broke me. He broke me and it took a long time to pick myself back up. Then entered Luke, who turned my world upside down and we became something special. Marrying right out of university.

"Well, hopefully you guys can work together, and you know, don't cause a hostile work environment for everyone else."

"I'm sure we will be fine, don't worry."

It was always nice to catch up with Crystal, she was my best friend. Thankfully, she knew to avoid the conversation about dead husbands and just kept it light-hearted. She wouldn't stop mentioning some new guy from across the street who had opened a bakery and how she'd already been there three times today to 'scope' the place out. She hated anything that drove her customers away and if the bakery started selling coffee, I knew she'd be out for blood.

"Do you think you will ever start dating again?" she asked me.

"Eh – Maybe, I mean, I don't know, it still feels too soon."

"It's been a year. Actually if we want to count it, fifteen months in fact Kim, and time heals all wounds. I'm not suggesting you just jump right into bed with someone, but go on a couple of dates, test the waters, you know. The pain won't last forever."

"My mom told me that and I know it won't be like this for years to come, but right now, it's still pretty raw."

"Well yeah, of course it is, but I know you will get through this. You're already doing so well, look at you back to work and you even came outside!"

She joked just as the bell above the café door rang. I knew it was him, even without looking. Daisy's ears went up and the look in Crystal's eyes gave it away. He was invading my space and I hated it.

"Evening, ladies," his voice, although friendly, a hint of flirting was hiding in it. "Can I sit anywhere?" Samuel directed his question to Crystal, who smiled her best hostess smile.

"Sure, let me grab you a menu."

She headed to the counter and waited for Samuel to take a seat on one of the counter stools before handing him the menu, patiently waiting for him to order something as I stared at his back.

"I'll have a cup of coffee and a slice of the pumpkin pie, please."

"Coming right up!"

I got the sense that Crystal was just happy a customer had come in, since the weather had become colder it was harder to get folks through the door. Unless it was quiz night or another event.

"So, come here as well do you?" He spun on his stool to face me and I quickly lowered my eyes. "First the rink and now here, aren't I lucky."

"It's a small town, you bump into all sorts here." I replied, drinking my coffee as Daisy stood up and placed her head on my lap.

"Is she yours?"

"Eh yeah, this is Daisy."

"German Shepherd, right?"

I nodded, rubbing behind Daisy's ear, begging Crystal to hurry up as I didn't fancy small talk. I just wanted to leave now, my comfort space was broken as soon as he arrived.

"Well, I best be off."

I said as I stood and started to put my coat on, just as Crystal reappeared. She placed Samuel's pie and coffee down in front of him and then caught sight of me and her eyes dropped. She didn't seem too happy with me suddenly leaving, but I was all peopled out for the day and just wanted my bed, a glass of red and something silly to watch on the television.

"Crys, I will text you later, thanks for the coffee."

"Alright, babes, get home safe."

We waved to each other and I left as quickly as I could, to stop any more conversations that I knew we may have had if I stuck around. They could catch up, that is if Samuel remembered Crystal, which was doubtful.

Opening the passenger door of my truck, Daisy jumped in knowing it was time to go home, to the comfort of my bed where I would fall asleep from the exhaustion of just existing. Luke would have been proud of me, for getting out of bed today and trying to put one foot in front of the other, no matter how difficult it was.

Once home, I texted Crystal to say I got home safely then decided I needed to hear my mom's voice. It had been a few days since we had a chat and I needed to talk to her.

"Hi, baby girl, are you ok?"

Instantly the wave of anxiety I had been fighting off fell from my shoulders, mom's voice working quickly. She didn't even have to say anything special.

"Hi, mom, I'm alright, I had my first day back at work today."

Filling up Daisy's food bowl and pouring myself a glass of wine as I held the phone between my ear and shoulder had become such a habit. I had always seemed to do a million things while on the phone and it always made Luke laugh. I would get myself so tangled carrying things while still trying to continue a conversation.

"Oh, well done! How did it go?"

"It was good actually, the new team is a bunch of teenage girls, so wish me luck with that - But they all have talent. I'm looking forward to seeing what they can do."

Slumping onto my sofa as I turned on the electric fireplace and pulled a blanket over my legs, I got comfortable as I waited for her reply.

"I saw that Jones's boy is back in town."

Of course, she had already heard, mom knew everything, she was part of the local church, the PTA, the neighborhood watch and the supermarket clerk most likely spilled the beans when she spotted him driving through town, this morning. Most likely how Crystal knew as well.

She knew of our history, and had always hated him, or at least that's what she told my seventeen-year-old self when he broke my heart.

"Yeah, I saw him, twice actually."

"You did!?" She shouted and I had to pull the phone away from my ear a little.

"Where?"

"Mom, inside voice."

"Sorry. But, please explain."

"He was at the rink this morning, offering to train the kids' ice-hockey team then again earlier at Crystal's café. I didn't stay long for a chat."

"Well, you stay one hundred feet away from that man you hear me. I won't have him trying to worm his way back into your life after what he did."

"Mom, that was years ago, it's long forgotten, and anyway, it will be hard to stay away from him when he's at my place of work four times a week."

She sighed and I heard her gulp back some of her drink, most likely drinking wine as well. We may have been mother and daughter, but we were also the best of friends. I told my mother everything and she had been my rock during Luke's passing.

"Well, anyways, your father wants to know are you coming to dinner this weekend?"

"Sure, Sunday, ok?"

"Sunday is perfect! We look forward to it, now get some shut eye, I bet you're tired from today. I have an early morning planned, the girls and I are meeting to go for a morning walk."

After saying goodnight and our I love you's, I called Daisy to follow me upstairs and I climbed into bed, knowing full well she would sleep on the bottom curled up against the back of my legs. Luke's side was still untouched and undisturbed, it may have looked funny to anyone on the outside, but I hated sleeping on his side as it never felt right.

"Goodnight, Daisy."

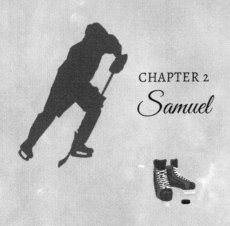

Tossing my rucksack onto the B&B bed, I flopped on the edge of it rubbing my face in my hands. I didn't want to be here, this was the last place I wanted to be sent, but my manager, Chris and his team of bitches didn't give a rats ass about my feelings. So off they boarded me onto a plane and well, here I am in the tiniest bedroom with a leaky tap in the bathroom. Great.

Seeing Kim was a surprise to say the least, but not that much of a shock. She hadn't changed, and I doubt she ever truly would. And of course, after she graduated from university she ended up back here, everybody did. Well, not me, I avoided this place like the plague.

I had yet to tell mom and dad I was back in town, but I knew one way or another they already knew. The church goers in this town were the biggest gossips I had ever come across, worse than the journalists I tussled with. Honestly, I didn't want them to know and I didn't fancy bumping into them either. They were the main reason I hated coming back here.

Glancing at the alarm clock, it was just past six and I didn't think it would be much fun to just sit here and wallow in self-pity, I had a better chance of doing that at a bar. And since this place was in the middle of town, I had the pickings of many places to hide out in.

Putting on my black leather wool lined jacket and wooly hat, I headed down main street, keeping my head low and my jacket collar up high, so no one would try to stop me to say hello or notice I was really here. I wanted to keep a low profile as best as I could. Rachel at the rink knew that she had to sign an NDA before I arrived, but there is no way a whole town would do that.

Especially, a town that hated me. A town that was happy to be rid of me, even if I was a star athlete and brought a lot of tourism to its door. The mayor, the police chief, and everyone else of authority hated me. But then, who could blame them? I was the worst kind of kid in a small town like this and when everyone found out what I did to good old Noah Morgan's daughter, well that just made matters worse.

I did so many awful things, treated people as if they were easily replaced. I treated Kimberly like a puppet on a string and would enjoy watching her dance and do everything I asked, and for what? Five minutes of my attention? I was such a jerk. When deep down, I was pretty sure I loved her, in that teenager 'bully the girl' you like kind of way. Breaking her heart was the worst thing I could ever have done and I have had to live with that ever since.

Spotting a lit-up café near the entrance of the town park, I could see a few bodies in the window and although I wanted something stronger to drink, a regular coffee and maybe some food might help get me out of this mood.

Pushing open the door, it was to my delight I saw Kim sitting there along with a beautiful dog laying at her feet. She however didn't seem that pleased to see me and sure enough after exchanging a few short words, she left without even glancing back.

"Sorry about her, she's still getting used to people again." The café waitress joked as she topped off my cup of coffee.

"Ah, it's alright, people suck anyways. So, is this your place?"

I asked, trying to sound somewhat interested, but I could feel this weird pull, as if I wanted to run after Kimberly and ask if she was ok, which would have been weird and very stalker-like.

"You don't remember me do you?" The waitress leaned against the counter, and I tried desperately to remember who she was.

"Sorry, not a clue, love."

"Crystal, Crystal James. You and your so-called friends used to beat up my little brother, Jamie."

"Ah, yeah." Lowering my eyes, the flashback instantly hit me. And I felt ashamed for how much of a dick I was in school. "Jim-Jam, yeah, eh – sorry about that."

What kind of parents named their kid Jamie with the last name James? They were just asking for him to get bullied and well, I wasn't a nice guy back then, and a lot of kids had to deal with it. Karma did always manage to get me back though, and now I was trying to make up for my mistakes and apologize whenever I could.

"I'm sorry I was such a jerk back in high school. You were friends with Kim as well weren't you?"

"Still are and it's alright, it was a long time ago now."

She turned away and began to clear the table her and Kim had been sitting at, the café was seemingly as quiet as the town. It felt as if everyone had already gone to bed even though the night was still young. It was strange, I was used to much busier and noisier cities.

"Where is everyone by the way? Walking here, I barely bumped into anyone."

"It's Wednesday, most folks are either at church mass or I think the school is having a football game tonight. Other than that, I have no idea."

Wednesdays, the busiest time on the town's weekly calendar. I had forgotten that football was on a weekly basis against the other local schools in the district, and church, well church was always being held no matter the time of day or year.

"That makes sense, well thanks for the coffee and the pie, maybe I will become a regular customer." I smiled, downing the last drop of coffee, and stood to take my leave.

"I'm sure Kim will 'love' that." Crystal said, sarcastically as I opened the door and headed back out into the cold.

UNABLE TO FIND a decent bar on my journey back to the B&B, I stopped at a little supermarket that was still open and stocked up on as many snacks as I could possibly carry as well as a couple of beers. Heading up to my room, I was hopeful the owner wouldn't spot me sneaking in anything.

I knew if I went home, I would have an endless supply of beers and all the food I wanted. Mom being the feeder she was, but I just didn't want to face the disappointment in dad's face when I told him why I am on leave.

It wasn't part of the plan he'd say, I should have done better, worked harder, worked until I was bleeding if it meant being at the top. A retired coach wasn't always the best parent to have, and poor mom just had to grin and bear the arguments and fights we'd get into.

I knew as soon as I left, Jane, my baby sister would have had to deal with his abuse and I tried so many times to reach out to her, to help her. After mom phoned me that night to tell me, Jane had run her car off Steel Bridge Road and didn't make it out of the water, I stayed away, kept myself busy, always blaming dad for putting his crap on Jane and me.

I should have been the big brother; I should have protected her. I didn't even attend her funeral, knowing full well I'd have killed him. Shaking my head of the thoughts as if they were still recent, but that was over five years ago. I just had to keep my head down, teach these kids and get back to my people, my team and away from him. Away from this town for good.

Throwing back my third can, I continued to flick through the TV watching the sports news as my team won another match against the US Giants and I felt sick when they mentioned that I was off with an injury, which of course was a lie. I had done all this to myself, and got too big for my boots. I'd heard my father's voice through my head when I hit Jason's face again and again, and again. He didn't deserve my attack, even if he did get in a number of punches himself. I should have known better and took care of my team, like a good captain.

I needed a break.

On a beach somewhere, in the sunshine with lots of girls in bikinis. Not in a shitty little town during fall. But again, here I am, painfully watching the interviews of my team's 'temporary captain'. Hearing my phone buzz gave me some small enjoyment until I started reading the notifications, not only had Jason, the temporary captain, taken my job, but he has also decided to take my locker room space, wear my jersey number '22' and was hitting on the girl I had been seeing, before being shipped off to this hellhole.

Tossing my phone across the room, it luckily landed into the armchair across from the bed, and did not break, thankfully. That would have just been another thing to piss me off for the day.

Rolling over and turning the TV off, I switched off the bedside lamp and tried to close my eyes. Sleep was always my only constant and of course, it is nowhere to be found now. Tossing and turning, back and forth for what felt like hours just got me riled up even more, but eventually sleep caught up with me and took me away.

CHAPTER 3
Kimberly

Training officially began and over the next few days, classes consisted of working on the girls' balance, spins and speed. And on how to work as a team and look after one another. It was interesting to say the least and even I was a bit rusty when I would show a move as an example. As the days went on, I didn't bump into Samuel, which was good. I didn't want to have any sort of conversations with him.

Luke's favorite time of year, Thanksgiving and the reminder of him hurt in my chest. His mom always made a maple and turkey roast, whereas his grandmother baked the best mincemeat and pumpkin pies you'd ever tasted.

They would of course expect me to come to dinner, to spend time with them, as I was still 'family', but I just couldn't face them, I wouldn't be able to put on some form of a smile and hide my emotions.

The radio in the rink had been really picking some songs today, all of which I tried to ignore until Lewis Capaldi's, "Wish You the Best", started to play and if it wasn't for the fact the girls were spinning and needed me to continue to be their spotter, I would had ran out of there as fast as my legs would take me.

I miss the green in your eyes...

Swallowing the lump that was forming in my throat as I fought back tears, Aimee, one of the girls, stopped dancing and looked at me with worry in her eyes. I tried to play it off as something in my eye and do that awkward smile you pull when you were trying not to cry. My chest was already tightening as it felt like the longest three minutes of my life. This song was played at his burial, and I could see it again in my mind, as the curtains closed around his coffin.

"Coach? Are you alright?"

All six girls stopped at once as Aimee spoke and every pair of eyes were on me and a small tear escaped, betraying me as my hands started to shake.

"Eh – Take five girls."

That voice. Samuel. And as much as I felt hatred towards him, I was grateful for his arrival as the girls nodded and skated off to the other side of the rink to catch five. He didn't put his hands on me, just stood behind me while I tried to catch my breath and stop my heart from racing.

"It's okay," his voice was assuring and calm.

Closing my eyes, I counted to ten, breathing in and out, the way my therapist had taught me. I thought the flashbacks had stopped, I thought I had moved past them, but sometimes, they come out of nowhere. Damn that song! Damn music and damn its way to break a person. Damn him for leaving me!

"I hate him," I whispered, "I hate him for leaving me here, alone."

"You're not alone, Kim, you are surrounded by many, that I'm sure love you."

"Ha, yeah, sure."

Finally, my breathing slowed to a normal pace as did my heart and I no longer felt the shaking, as well it would seem the music had been turned down. Looking across to the girls, I spotted Aimee still looking at me with a small smile on her face and no longer wearing her skates. Did she ask the front desk to turn it down? Maybe. Or maybe it was just my imagination.

Leaving Samuel and skating up to the girls. I felt a headache start to develop, as it always did after one of those episodes and I knew I wouldn't be fully on my game while I was like this.

"Thank you for today girls, you're all doing amazingly. Take this weekend off, we will pick back up on Monday after you finish school."

"Yes, Coach."

"Bye, Coach."

There was an echo of yeses and goodbyes as they all began to pack up their stuff and leave, all but for Aimee. She was waiting there patiently, as if she was eager to say something.

"When my me-ma died, I couldn't listen to certain songs either. I found that sometimes earplugs helped when I was out in public places, like the mall where they were always playing songs. It just made life a little easier."

She was so sweet and young, she should never have felt any of the pain you were cursed with when a loved one died. Smiling an easier smile than the one before, I took some comfort in her knowing exactly what had happened and the fact I had a group of girls who were a delight to teach.

"Thank you, Aimee, enjoy your weekend."

"Thanks, Coach."

By the time I had turned around, Samuel was gone, and I

felt my chest sigh. In relief? Or maybe a little hidden disappointment? He didn't have to come and help me, he could have just gone on with his day and I would have been fine, I was always fine.

Packing up my things and heading to my truck, the sun was starting to set, and that beautiful, orange-pink glow was falling across the sky. Gorgeous. I decided to head to mom's on the way out of the rink for dinner, it had been a while and I knew if I didn't show up soon she would nag me to death.

Crystal and I had plans for later in the night, to head to one of the town's bars and enjoy a few beers together, maybe play some pool or have a game of darts, like old times.

I was so desperate to get back to who I used to be, before Luke, but I think that person was long gone now and I had to accept that. I needed to find out who I was now. I didn't want to sit in this pit of darkness for the rest of my life, being overcome by grief to the point I couldn't move forward.

That wouldn't have been what Luke wanted for me. He wanted me to be happy, to continue on with my life and I hated him for it. How was I meant to continue without him?

Not worrying about Daisy as I already had the dog walker in twice during the day, an automatic feeder and Netflix playing all day, I knew she was living the life of luxury while I waited for the million questions my mom would fire at me over a glass of wine at the dinner table.

As dad topped off mom's glass, then handed me the bottle of red, he smiled at me with that awkward 'good luck' smile.

Mom came in holding a plate in each hand, setting dinner down in front of us first then went back into the kitchen to get her plate.

"Joseph will be coming soon with Bethan."

"I didn't think Joe was back from base yet?" I asked, as mom pulled her chair in.

"He got back a few days ago, he's been staying with Bethan at her parents. He said he has some news to tell us."

"Watch him tell us he's knocked her up."

"Noah you can't say things like that at the dinner table and besides Joseph is a good boy."

Dinner was quiet after mom scolded dad, other than the odd question about my team, how dad's retirement was working out for him and mom deciding she wanted to learn how to paint. Joseph hadn't returned my text, the one I sneakily sent from under the table asking for some clue as to whatever this news was. What was worse, Joseph and Bethan didn't arrive until we were cleaning up the table, making us wait longer than expected.

"As always, you arrive after it's time to clear up."

Mom joked as she wrapped her arms around his neck and gave him a kiss on the cheek and then did the same to Bethan.

"It's so lovely to have you home," dad shouted over the sound of tonight's sports news.

"Yes, well, like I said over the phone earlier mom I – we have some news we would like to tell you."

I stood in the doorway of the living room as I came back in from topping up my glass and Bethan looked as if she was ready to burst from excitement. The four of them looked at me as I walked in, clearly waiting for me. Taking my seat in the smaller armchair of the sofa set, I waited for the big announcement. I had a feeling I knew what was about to come.

"Mom, dad, Kimmy," Joseph paused, taking Bethan's hands in his and then looked back at us smiling again, "I asked Bethan to marry me and - She said yes!"

Mom was the first one to scream in excitement and fill the room instantly with joy, dad was on his feet in an instant embracing Joe in a hug. And then mom was fawning over Bethan's ring, a beautiful diamond ring that sparkled in the living room lights.

"Oh, it's beautiful – oh I'm so happy."

Mom's chorus of delights and joyfulness continued for a few minutes until I felt their eyes back on me. I hadn't said a word as the news settled, I remembered that feeling of happiness, sharing that news and excitement with my family and friends. I liked Beth, she and Joseph had been together since right after high school. She's stuck by him throughout his military training, deployments and everything else in between. They were perfect for each other; she was a little timid, while he was the wild second child. They balanced each other out.

"Kimmy? Do you approve?" Joe sat next to me with his hand on my knee, looking at me with hopeful eyes.

"Of course – of course I'm happy. Why wouldn't I approve?"

I shot the biggest, happiest smile I could muster towards him and Beth, bringing him in for a hug as I buried my feelings deep inside myself. I would cry at home. Not now. I wouldn't ruin this moment for them both.

"Good, cause I need you to be my best man or best woman, sorry."

"You are joking right? Have one of your army guys be your best man, not me."

"Kim, you're my sister and my best friend. Plus, you're the

best person for the job. Don't fight me on this either. You need to bring a date as well"

A date? Panic ran through me, I didn't even know a guy to bring to a wedding. I would just be happy to be by myself. I expected Joe to wear his Mess dress uniform, along with his friends. While Bethan and her girlfriends walk down the aisle, looking like they all stepped out of a fairytale. However, I wouldn't have any idea what type of suit I'd wear.

"Don't worry either, Beth said you don't have to wear a suit." It was as if he read my mind.

"Yeah Kim, if you'd like to wear a dress, please do."

This made me a little more relaxed, I never got to dress up anymore, so wearing a nice formal dress for my little brother's wedding was something I really wanted to do.

"Oh, mom, there's one more thing."

"You're not pregnant are you?" Dad shot Beth and Joe a look of 'please dear Lord no' and Beth laughed uncomfortably.

"No! No, haha, no. Ummm," Joe was starting to stumble over his words, like he did when he was embarrassed and beginning to feel overwhelmed.

"We'd like to be married at the end of November," Bethan said for her soon to be husband, in her quiet nervous voice.

"NOVEMBER!?" Mom shouted.

"Yes, I know it's only about two months away, but I always pictured myself getting married around Christmas time with the fairy lights and Christmas trees. We could do that, right, can't we?"

Mom looked at me with panic in her eyes and I already saw the sweat beginning to appear on her forehead. When I married Luke, our wedding was a small summer time ceremony and we had about six months to plan. However, to only have two months to plan a wedding, that would be a challenge, but not impossible, not while mom and I got to organize it.

"Mom and I will help every way we can." I interrupt, not even knowing why I offered to help other than the look of gratitude from them both.

WE HAD dessert and another bottle of wine to celebrate. When I heard my phone ringing from the dining room, I suspected it was Crystal, most likely wondering where I was and when I would be joining her and the other girls for drinks. I hadn't realized that time had marched on, it was coming close to nine at night. Bethan, mom, and I had been chatting about what colors she and Joe would like, the style of dress she wanted to wear and if she had already picked out her bridesmaids.

Joe had also decided that my sweet Daisy was to be their ring-bearer. Which of course was going to be quite funny as she would most likely ignore his calls to walk down the aisle or would get too distracted by the pretty lights. Nevertheless, we would work with what they wanted.

"Do you need a lift?"

Dad asked as he spotted me leaning against the dining table flicking through messages on my phone.

"You sure?"

"Anything for my girl."

Smiling at dad, I grabbed my things and said my goodbyes before jumping into the passenger side of his truck and headed into town. Everyone drove some form of four-by-four here as it was the best to use whenever we had snow. But this year, it hadn't arrived yet, so we were all just waiting for the cold to appear.

"How are you feeling?" Dad asked me as I continued to stare out the window.

"I'm fine, why wouldn't I be?"

"Well, I remember when you and Luke told us you were getting married and how happy you both were. Must be hard seeing your brother having his turn now."

"Joe deserves to be happy and to feel that excitement. Beth is family already and honestly, I'm fine."

I had gotten so used to telling people that I was okay when really I wasn't. That it was just an automatic response at this point. I didn't believe my own words. But, I was happy that Joe found the person he wanted to spend the rest of his life with. As his big sister it had always been my job to look out for him, but to also stand by him whatever he decided to do in life and my grief wouldn't stop that.

"Well, you're still my little girl and I am only a phone call away if you want to talk."

"I know dad, but honestly, I'm fine. I'm more concerned about the fact that Joe wants me to bring a date and I have no people skills for picking up guys at bars. Nor am I ready, or would even want to bring a random bar guy as my date."

"Ahh, you will figure it out, you always do."

He was right, in some way, I had always had a way of figuring things out and if push came to shove I'd ask Crystal to be my date. Even if I now had to beg her to bake the wedding cake and help us with the catering for the reception. She had grown up with Joe and I, so it only seemed right I'd at least ask her to help my brother, Joe.

I was grateful she was in the business of hospitality. Her cooking was incredible. Maybe I would suggest to her to expand her business one day and offer functions at the café, maybe as she had a knack for it.

As dad pulled up outside *The Silver Cat Bar & Grill*, Crystal was waiting outside for me as well as chatting to the bouncer. Kissing dad on the cheek before jumping out, I hurried to meet up with her. After she smiled and waved at him, we headed inside.

CHAPTER 4
Kimberly

The bar was one of the newer, updated buildings in town. It had sections within that weren't all about blasting music. Instead it had areas that had board games, pool tables, dart boards, a hookah lounge as well as a small dance section with a DJ. It had quickly become one of mine and Crystal's favorite places to go once it opened and it became our normal hangout.

"I need a drink."

Those were the first words that came out of my mouth as we reached the other girls. The Coven, as she would call them. They had all been to something called a spiritual awakening and the end result demanded beer and thus our night out had been planned ahead.

"Everything alright?" Crystal asked me as I threw back my second shot of tequila.

"My brother is getting married."

I tapped the bar and the waitress poured me another shot. I normally stuck to drinking wine, but tonight it was the stronger stuff that was needed. The last time I drank anything like this was after Luke's death. But now, I was stressed and drinking tequila as if it was the last drink in the world.

"And that's a bad thing?" Crystal replied, taking a swig of her beer.

"No, it's not, it's just..."

Why was I feeling upset? I had been fine, well as fine as I could be while we discussed his wedding plans. Maybe it was the fact I was being reminded of Luke at every turn today. Maybe it was the left-over emotions I had from earlier at the rink?

"I'm Joe's best man and I've been ordered to find a date."

"That's awesome! And so easy to fix, let's have a look around for some good-looking men and see what we can do."

Linking her arm in mine, she twirled me around and we headed to the table where the girls were all sitting. Jasmine, the tallest and loudest of the group, was already jumping from her seat and waving at me. Lacy, the beautiful, curvy, bright blue haired, tattooed one waved at me gently.

Whilst Megan was shuffling a pack of tarot cards as Crystal shoved me down into the seat next to her and took her own seat next to Lacy. Crystal brushed a strand of hair from Lacy's face, both of them shone with their love for one another.

Crystal had come out to me back in our early teens about being bisexual and she had been seeing Lacy for the last two years. It had been kept quiet at the start, especially with the town filled with people who were against anything other than heterosexual love. However, when their relationship did become public, it was received with kindness.

Lacy looked at Crystal the way anyone would wish to be looked at. The love and adoration in her eyes made me smile. I was so happy my bestie had found her person, but also slightly jealous they had this together.

"Our little Kim needs a date for her brother's wedding."

"Baby bro is getting married!? That's awesome!!" Jasmine exclaimed as she shouted and waved the waitress over. "More beers please, Jen, we have some things we need to celebrate!"

Jasmine, although loud and out there, was an amazing person and friend. When Crystal wasn't able to visit us at the hospital during Luke's treatments, Jasmine would come in her place with bags of fresh, clean clothes, snacks, and anything we needed. Those four had become my family during that time and beyond.

"We have two months to plan everything. Crys, can you bake them a cake please? A Christmas themed one and eh – would you also be able to help with the catering?"

"We will all help! You don't even have to ask." Lacy interrupted before Crystal could give an answer.

"What kind of date do you want then, Kimmy?" Jasmine asked as she helped the waitress take off the bottles of beer on the tray.

"Oh, God, I don't know. It's been so long since I had to flirt with another human being, so if I can't find anyone either one of you or Crystal will be my date."

The four of them chuckled in response. The evening continued on, and we carried on drinking more beers, played a few games of pool and danced to some cheesy '90s tunes that the DJ had thought would be entertaining to play.

Lacy and Crystal had scurried off outside to have a cigarette. Megan was throwing darts clearly picturing her ex-husband's face on the board. While Jasmine and I sat and talked about life.

"How's work going?"

"It's going ok, the new team of girls I've got are lovely and great to teach. Rachel, my manager is just letting me get on with things and not breathing down my neck, which makes a change."

"Well, of course she is leaving you alone, no offence babes, but everyone is still afraid of upsetting you."

A dart flew towards the board Megan was using and it almost felt as if it landed in my chest. Ouch. Jasmine's words threw me a little as I had been trying so hard to appear fine, to not let things people said get to me and to just continue on with my life, as normal as possible.

"I don't mean that in a nasty way, it's just everyone knows what happened and well, some of them don't want you to break."

"Right, well I'm fine and not going to break. I am trying to move forward with my life, it's what Luke would have wanted."

Grief was such an ugly emotion to have, it didn't define who I was as a person either. I was still Kimberly, a world champion figure skater. I just had to retire early to take care of Luke and I was fine with that. It just meant now that he was gone, I had to find out who I was and not just who I used to be.

"What about him?"

Jasmine brought me back to our surroundings and I looked to where she was pointing at the guy leaning against the bar who just happened to be looking at me.

And of course, it was Samuel.

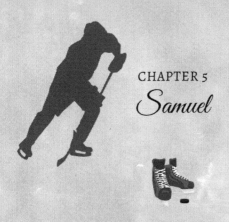

I spotted her the moment I walked into the bar. It was as if I were the moth to her flame. It was hard not to have noticed her table, which was filled with other women when I walked by, heading towards the bar. I had not expected it to be as busy as it was.

The whole new concept of bars having 'quiet' areas as well as game sections and dancing sections had hit mainstream Vancouver a year or so ago. And this was the first time I had stepped into a bar like this. I normally did my best to avoid them.

After the phone call I had with my manager this evening demanding I get out and socialize, I now found myself sitting at the bar with my Vancouver Devils cap on, hoping no one would recognize who I am.

Of course, after a few minutes some guy and his buddies made their way over to me. They asked if I was really Samuel Jones and why I had not played in last night's game. Giving them the PR crap my team had given me, it seemed to satisfy them, thankfully. I didn't want a PR issue.

We took a few selfies and a shot of whiskey together before

they were shooed away by the bartender. Grateful for him telling them to piss off, I made a mental note to remember to tip him very well.

Kimberly seemed to be having fun with her girlfriends. It was nice to see considering what had happened at the rink today. I would have liked to stay with her earlier, asked if she was alright, but it felt like it wasn't my place after she had skated off.

The salty taste of beer hit my lips and I just sit in silence. Oddly enjoying the noises of everyone around me as they laughed, joked, and danced with friends. It was a Friday night and people were not only playing darts and pool, but also board games.

Looking up again, I saw one of Kimberly's friends was staring at me then she caught my eye. *Shit.* I didn't want her thinking I was looking at her. I was not being a creepy guy, but now I couldn't take my eyes off her.

She was wearing a low-cut black top that showed off her collarbones and the tightest pair of jeans I had ever seen her in, paired with some sexy as hell heels. Shaking my head, I looked away and took a sip of my drink. I had suddenly developed a dry mouth.

"I thought you didn't like people."

She took me by surprise as she leaned against the bar beside me, waving the bartender over.

"The same again, for me and my ladies, please, Josh?"

She smiled sweetly, but I knew she was trying to keep herself from breaking. I knew Kim better than anyone, well I used to know her better than everyone, now I wasn't so sure. So much had changed.

"I sometimes like to come out of my cave and besides, the beer is better here than the crap I bought at the market."

"Ah, yes, Josh does have the best on tap. Well, enjoy your evening."

She paid for her drinks then proceeded to carry the tray over to the table. For a split second I thought about getting up to offer her a hand, but I had to stop myself. I didn't want to insert myself too much into her life. After what I did, I didn't speak to her and well, I ignored her like the asshole I was.

"Say," she paused, turning back to me, "would you like to join us? It would save you from getting cornered by all the men in here who are dying to speak to you and all the single ladies from trying to hook up with you, unless that's what you want?"

She was asking me to join her. That was quite an unexpected surprise, as I was starting to think the only reason she spoke to me was because we had been stuck at the rink together.

"Won't I be disturbing your girls-night?" I asked, wondering if she was joking.

"It was Jasmine's suggestion, she said you were looking pretty lonely over here."

"Well, in that case, sure."

Taking hold of the tray of drinks and putting mine on there, I followed her over to the table and placed the tray down. I felt a bit surprised that they even suggested I come and sit with them. That's when I sensed it. This might have been a bad idea.

"Everyone, this is Samuel. Sam, this is Jasmine, Megan, Lacy, and I believe you've already met Crystal."

"Eh – Nice to meet you all."

I was feeling a little sheepish as I took my seat next to Kimberly, the only space that appeared to be free. It was a bit snugged as the booth was pretty full by the other four ladies. Crystal, and I believed her name was Lacy, went back to their conversation. The girl with short brown hair, sitting opposite of me, was playing with a deck of tarot cards and the one next to her, the tallest, was smiling at me a little too happily.

"Kim says you went to school together?" The smiling one asked me.

"Oh, eh yeah, she was in the year below me. If it wasn't for Kim I would have failed science."

"And math." Kim took a sip of her drink smiling at me.

"And math."

"Oh, and don't forget you tutored him in English studies." Crystal jumped in and I felt my cheeks go a little red.

"Yep, I was a pretty bad student. I was too busy playing hockey to care about studying. Kim was asked to be my tutor as she was at the top of her class in everything."

I was arrogant and didn't care that I was failing any of my classes. Grades didn't matter, I just wanted to play sports, but she soon sorted me out. She had gleefully ripped me a new one whenever she could. When I got my first B minus I remembered her celebrating and giving me the biggest gold star sticker I had ever seen. I still had it, back at home, stuffed in a drawer somewhere with that B minus paper.

"If it wasn't for Kim, I wouldn't have been able to pass high school and get my scholarship. I owe it all to her really."

She suddenly looked embarrassed, quickly excusing herself. Kim ran off with the taller girl following her to the bathroom. Turning back to the table feeling confused, I noticed Crystal and her date looked at me with a hint of anger in their eyes.

"That was also when you dumped her after promising to take her to prom," Crystal snapped.

I hadn't forgotten what I did. Truth was, I didn't get to go to that prom, but that was a whole different story that I hoped to be able to tell Kimberly one day. Crystal's date put her hand on hers and they both left the table. Clearly I have left a sour taste in everyone's mouth.

"Don't worry about it." The girl with cards speaks up. "They are just overprotective of Kim, she'll be fine. The cards tell me you have a long road ahead of you both, are you ready to share it together?"

"I'm sorry, I don't believe in that sort of stuff."

I didn't. I was never someone who would be fooled by horoscopes or the universe telling you karma is real. But then again I am pretty sure karma was kicking my ass at this very moment.

"It doesn't matter if you believe in it or not, you being here was meant to be."

"Hmmm, we will see if Kimberly believes that. I should leave you girls for the rest of your evening, I've gate crashed long enough."

Swigging back my drink and getting up to head back to my spot on the bar, I'm suddenly stopped. Crystal, her date, Kimberly and the tall one stood before me, almost in a protective circle around Kimberly and I knew it was because of me.

"Ok, we have come up with a plan of how you can make it up to Kim for ditching her that night," Crystal said with an attitude, crossing her arms and cocking her hip.

"Go on..." I was intrigued by whatever they had planned.

Kimberly didn't seem to be impressed, keeping her eyes on the floor, refusing to meet mine. "Girls, please just leave it."

"No, he owes you one. So, Samuel, you will be Kim's date to her brother's wedding and if you screw up, we will set all hell loose upon you."

"Wait, what!?"

Kim pulled the tall one back and looked up at her with wide eyes. I don't think this was the plan they had suggested to her back in the bathroom. She finally looks at me then back at her friends, and I just stood there unsure of what I was supposed to say. Yes, sure, of course I'd be her date, I'd happily be her date! But I couldn't very well say that judging by her reaction.

"Jaz, that's not what we discussed. I just wanted an apology."

"Yes, but now you can solve two problems."

"My mother still wants to kill him, so I don't think it would be a good idea."

"Then invite him round to dinner with your parents and you guys can clear the air, but one way or another, he's your date."

Jasmine appeared to be the ringleader of them all and a part of me wanted to high five her. This would not only give me the chance to spend some time with Kimberly, but I'd also get to explain everything.

I would tell her why I did what I did, and why she didn't go to prom with me. I owed her an explanation and even if it was about ten years late, but it was better late than never.

"If it's alright with you Kim, I'm happy to help anyway I can."

She sighed, rolling her eyes at me, and pushed past her friends. Suddenly leaving the bar, she grabbed her coat on the way out. Her friends all looked at me as if to say it was my job to go after her. Part of me wanted to, but I also felt super awkward at the thought of chasing after her. It was my being here that had caused this issue in the first place.

Puffing out a sigh, I grabbed my coat and followed her out into the cold.

CHAPTER 6
Kimberly

Out of all the stunts they could have pulled, this was one of the worst. The cold brisk air wrapped itself around me as I pushed the door open and entered the quiet and dimly lit street. Crossing my arms, trying to keep some heat in. I started to walk as fast as my legs would take me, it would take a while to get home, but I'd get there. Eventually.

"Kimberly!"

Anger bellowed in the pit of my stomach as his voice rang through the air. I wanted to punch him. I was trying to get away from my past, but it was always trying to run up and attack me. Luke was still meant to be here and if he was, I wouldn't have to deal with any of this. I wouldn't need to find a date for my brother's wedding. He was meant to be my date till the day I died.

"Go away, Sam!" I shouted, picking up my pace.

"You will freeze if you walk home. Come on, let me drive you, my car is just across the road and I only had one beer."

"Look."

Stopping and turning to him suddenly, my voice caught in

my throat as I looked at him, helpless as he held out his jacket to me.

"Sam, you don't have to pretend to be nice to me. You don't have to be my date either, I will do just fine on my own."

"I have no doubt you will do 'just fine', but honestly let me at least help you by taking you home. I will even drop you off at the end of your street if you don't want me to know which house is yours."

He sounded slightly desperate and as if he was clinging to something. The anger in the pit of my stomach turned to flutters. Luke's face flashed in my mind as I reached out for Sam's jacket. I was cold, and he didn't seem to mind it. Hockey players very rarely felt the cold; lucky them.

"Please, Kim, I don't want you to walk home and plus if I go back in there, your friends will probably murder me."

I laughed a little knowing full well, they'd tell him off for letting me get away. I could understand his hesitation as they could be scary, especially when all four of them were coming at you like banshees.

Putting his much larger jacket on, it almost drowned me. And I saw he was trying not to laugh at me. He still smelled of Hugo Boss aftershave and peppermint toothpaste. Some things never changed.

"Alright, fine, you can give me a ride home."

"Great! Stay here, I will bring the car round."

Rushing off then, he disappears across the street and down a side street. For a few minutes I was alone, until the roar of an engine filled the quiet street. A brand-new silver Mercedes came to a halt. Getting out from his driver's side, he rushed around and opened the passenger door for me, attempting to be a gentleman. The heat was already blowing and he buckled himself in. We sat there for a moment in silence.

"Eh, where'd you live?"

"Just off Bailey and Brook Road. Number twenty-two."

"Oh! That's the pink house, isn't it?"

"That's my neighbor, I'm the boring white one with the wrap-around porch."

We sat in silence again, feeling awkward; I was unsure of what to say or if I should even say anything. The radio was on low, and I'm pretty sure "Teenage Dirtbag" was playing. Then as if he read my mind, he slowly turned up the volume.

"Ahaha! Do you remember this song? God, that was a long time ago."

"Early 2000s I think. And I'm pretty sure I still remember all the words."

This was the only song I would stand that Samuel would often blast during our study sessions. Pretending to play air guitar and no matter how many times I would have told him to get off the table, he continued and would always attempt to get me up with him to sing.

"OH, WEEEEEE YEAHHHH!! DIRTBAG!!"

He started to sing loudly, and I shook my head in second-hand embarrassment for him.

"Come on, Kimmy!"

Rubbing my hand on my face, I laughed listening to him sing out of tune as he started the verse about prom and Iron Maiden. I always pictured this song playing during our prom and he, my date, would have sung this to me.

It was then I realized, this was the first time I had heard the song since he broke up with me. Even during mine and Luke's wedding day, I had banned it from our DJ list. Music always had a way of playing with your emotions and bringing you back to moments in your life you'd forgotten. It was the the power of music, Luke would have said.

"Listen, Kim."

"We're here."

I interrupted him, not sure if I wanted him to continue what he was going to say. I was out of the car before he could finish his sentence, fishing for my front door keys in my handbag.

"Thank you for the lift." I shouted just loud enough for him to hear me.

Opening and shutting the door quickly behind me, Daisy rushed to greet me, but I acknowledge her only for a second. Before rushing to stare out from the front door window. Waiting to see through the fogged glass for him to turn his car around and drive off. A sigh of relief escaped me, then the cry I have been holding in since the song started.

"Alexa, play Lana Del Rey."

As music had already destroyed my day, reminding me of things I didn't want to be reminded of, I might as well play one of my favorite artists. "Say Yes To Heaven" started to play throughout the house. Luke had set up speakers in every room connecting to our living rooms Alexa. He said it was a way to create magic wherever you went. He had such an ear for lyrics and melodies, if the cancer hadn't taken him, he was going to become a composer and he would have made an amazing career of it.

Giving Daisy a hug and a kiss as she had waited patiently for me. Finally I locked the front door and headed towards the kitchen. I needed another drink and the wine in the fridge was calling to me as my phone buzzed.

Did you get home safe?

It was a message in our group chat from Jasmine. Instead of answering I flicked my phone face down. I refused to answer it yet. But before I knew it, it buzzed again, and again and again. More texts from the other girls.

Oi. Don't ignore us.

We will continue to bother you until you answer.

Or we will phone the sheriff to come check on you.

Alright Jaz!

Yes, I'm home safe and sound. Sam gave me a ride.

Did you ride him to? ;)

You're disgusting,

And no, he dropped me at the bottom of my drive, I said thanks and left.

Filling my glass halfway then grabbing a dog treat for Daisy, I headed to my sofa. Switching the fire on via the remote, I was grateful for the instant warmth it gave the room.

Another buzz and this time it wasn't from the group chat, but an unknown number.

Hey! Sorry if I made you feel awkward earlier.

Who's this?

Sam. Sorry, my PA gave me your number.

And how the hell did your PA get my number?

Ah, eh, you know I didn't think to ask her. Sorry, should I delete it?

Well, this felt like an invasion of privacy if I ever saw it. I was ready to angrily text back demanding he removed my number from his phone, but something stopped me. Looking down at Daisy, she came up to sit next to me on the sofa, tucking her nose in my lap. She looked up at me with her beautiful brown eyes just begging for ear scratches.

Looking away from her puppy dog eyes, my eyes fell on the only photograph of Luke and I that was left on the mantelpiece. The photograph was of us in the snow, I was on top of his back and both of us were beaming with smiles. Daisy, who was only a year old at the time, was laying at our feet.

> No, it's fine. You didn't make me feel awkward, that song just brings back memories, that's all.

> Good ones, I hope.

> Hmm

> Thanks again for the lift.

> It's all good. Do you need a lift to pick up your car tomorrow?

> It's at my parents' house, my brother and dad will drop it tomorrow, I think.

Watching as the typing bubble came up then stopped, I looked at it for a few more seconds before putting my phone down. The conversation couldn't go anywhere after that. Which I was fine with, wasn't I? This was Sam, the guy who pretty much broke my heart and left me for dead.

It took me a long time to repair myself; a young teenager and her first love. He just stopped, didn't return my calls or my texts and I never found out why. So, as any normal teenage girl would have done, I blamed myself.

I changed myself, my hair, the way I dressed, the way I spoke, I even started to lose weight, thinking that these were all the reasons he just stopped. And now, I was feeling like that girl again, waiting on bated breath for him to text me back. Idiot.

Switching my phone to do not disturb, I finished my drink and headed to bed. I had planned to get up early and head down to the rink to skate before anyone got there, but that was before I drank too much out with the girls. A sleep in would be lovely, leaving my phone downstairs and turning off my alarms on Alexa, we headed to bed and instead of music, rain sounds played throughout the house.

SLEEPING in on a Sunday was always one of my favorite things to do and after tossing and turning all night as I had, it was needed. The teenager in me was screaming and shouting at me, to go grab my phone. I had to fight the urge so many times, to keep from pulling back the covers and rushing downstairs.

When I did eventually venture down, I let Daisy out first then put on a pot of coffee. The morning never started unless coffee was made. It was only then after putting a throw across my shoulders did I take my phone and head out to sit on the porch.

The morning dew was still clinging to the grass outside, and I could see my breath while the leaves began to fall from the trees, the beautiful cul-de-sac filled with a mixture of oranges, greens, and yellows. Each house was decorated already for Halloween, which was only a week or so away then it would be Christmas lights galore. I had yet to decorate my porch for the festivities and I knew if I didn't, the neighborhood watch would be on my case. We had an image to keep up and I couldn't let them down.

Making a mental note, I made a plan to head to the small Target we had and a few other little stores to buy some decorations. I had already checked and saw that my brother and dad had already dropped my car back off.

Turning my phone off silent, I went straight to my Facebook messages and found Bethan. It would be a good idea for her to come with me, as we needed things to decorate my parents' garden and get it ready for the wedding reception.

Waiting for her to message back, I looked at my notifications. Avoiding my texts at all costs, I answered a few emails instead before eventually having a quick glance and there were two notifications, from Samuel.

> If you're not busy tomorrow, and if you still want me to be your date.

> I will need a suit, so would you be up for helping pick a suit, one that maybe will match your dress or something?

Another text.

> That is if you want to match obv. Let me know. We could grab lunch?

> Or not.

> Yeah.

> Ummm.

> Let me know when you can, if you know, you want to obviously. No pressure!

Reading those chaotic texts made me laugh a little, as they read as if he had sent the one text then regretted it and sent another then regretted that one, too. As if we were still in high school. I had half a mind to not message him back as it was a Sunday, and I doubted any shops that sell suits would be open. Perhaps tomorrow before practice we could maybe go.

Maybe.

> Hi Sam, no suit shops are open on Sunday, so maybe tomorrow we can go to a place I know. As for grabbing lunch, we shall see how tomorrow goes. Before practice would be better, I have a class at two o'clock. Let me know.

Finishing my coffee and heading upstairs to get dressed and prepared for the day, I waited patiently for Bethan to respond and once the hour mark hit, I decided to just go to Target myself and see what I could find that perhaps would work for the wedding and for decorating my house.

"Afternoon, Mrs. St. Clair!"

Hearing my husband's last name took me by surprise as it was not something I was expecting to hear this morning and the fact I had gone back to using my maiden name since Luke died.

Turning around I found the two girl scouts of my small area standing at the bottom of my porch steps. And a fake smile showed up on my face as I kicked myself. I was usually pretty good at avoiding them, but not today.

"We are raising funds for the girl scouts Christmas party and for the local elderly home, would you like to buy some cookies?"

"Oh, sorry girls, I'm on a no sugar diet," I lied.

"They are completely sugar, gluten, egg and dairy free, so you should be fine."

"So, they have no real taste to them," I muttered. "Great, I am on my way out though girls so if you could come back tomorrow, I can pay you then."

"Sure thing, Mrs. St. Clair! Thank you."

As they skipped away, I rubbed my forehead as I knew they would be after more than one box payment tomorrow. I guess I would be stuck with cardboard tasting cookies. Just as I locked the front door, I felt my phone start to vibrate then ring as the name Samuel popped up on my screen.

Why did he have to call me? Why couldn't he text like a normal person? Leaving it to ring a few more seconds, I reluctantly answered it.

"Hey, sorry, am I calling at a bad time?"

"No, it's fine I was just getting in the car. Let me hook it up to Bluetooth."

Waiting for a minute or two as my phone connected to the car, I didn't know if he had hung up or was still waiting patiently.

"Are you still there?" I asked.

"Yeah, yeah, so, I found a suit shop in Caulfeild that's open. Well, they weren't, but when I phoned my team and told them I needed a suit, they called *Henry Rosen*, I think is the name of the shop, and they, eh, said they'd open for me."

Turning down Moreland drive and heading to the B7 route towards Target, I had to pull over in a small layby to concentrate. Did he actually say the store had opened on its day off just for him? For him to have a suit for my brother's wedding? Somewhere I was still unsure he should be coming to, especially considering my family already hated him.

"Let me get this straight, so because you're some hot shot hockey player, they are opening their store just for you."

"Oh, they sell dresses as well! And I may have mentioned you're my date."

I could hear the awkwardness in his voice as he waited for

me to perhaps shout at him, but all I could do was sigh. What was I getting myself into? I did need a dress, but I wasn't sure what Joseph wanted me to wear as I was his best man.

"Let me call you back. Give me five minutes."

Hanging up without protest, I counted to ten as my heart started to rapidly beat, the anxiety and panic trying to take over. I needed to talk to my brother before any of this suit and dress shopping business began as he was one of the guys Samuel would bully in school.

"Hey, big sis, what's up?"

He sounded as if he was back at our parents, as I was sure I could overhear dad in the background shouting about lunch or some sort of sandwich complaint.

"Can we talk?"

"We are talking," he joked.

"Joe, seriously, you alone?"

Waiting a second or two, I heard the porch side door open and close.

"I am now, what's the matter?"

"Okay, I have a date, kinda for your wedding and I need to know if I am wearing a dress, or you want me to wear a suit? Either way, have you and Bethan decided on a color scheme."

I was met with silence, and I wasn't sure how to take it, did the phone cut out? Joseph and Luke were great friends, and it broke me to phone him that day while he was away on duty. Telling him Luke had died and hearing him break on the other end of the phone would live with me forever.

"Beth said she'd like Christmas colors, so I guess, reds, greens, golds. You know more about this shit than I do, and she said you should wear a dress."

No comment about my date, I wasn't sure how I was meant to take that, but I didn't want to press any further.

"Kimmy, I gotta go. I think mom's just about to murder dad, call you later, ok."

Before I could answer, he hung up and my phone started to ring again. Sam.

"So, we on for today? Where shall I pick you up?"

"I will meet you at Crystal's café in ten minutes."

Rolling my eyes, I sighed. My day was already not going as I planned it to. I did a U-Turn and headed back into town, where I left my car outside Crystal's café. And now to wait for the awkward conversation that would ensue for the next hours' drive.

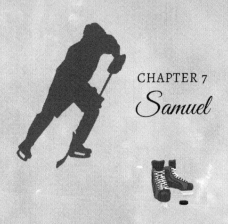

T hrowing a fist in the air as I quickly leaped from the bed and threw on a pair of jeans, gray t-shirt, and a brown cozy sweater, as it looked a bit chilly outside. I was finally going to speak to Kim without any interruptions and without any distractions, or her friends making it awkward.

I had already planned the day once Emily had called me back, having secured the store. Now if I could get Kim to try on a dress or two, and assuming she liked one, I would buy it for her in an instant. I had made reservations for a little café on the high street for later on in the day. I felt like a schoolboy, I was so excited to spend some time with her.

Rushing out of the B&B and jumping to my car, it was only a short drive toward Crystal's café. Pulling into the parking lot, I instantly saw Kim. She was leaning against the trunk of her car with her arms crossed and she didn't seem at all impressed.

Maybe I should have taken her lead and waited. I was just used to getting my way and getting things done as soon as I wanted them. I didn't really know how to hold back and wait.

As I undid my seatbelt, readying to get out to open the passenger door, she opened it with a bit of force and fell into her seat. Silently and forcefully doing her seatbelt up, she went back to looking at her phone. Something was occupying her brain, but I wasn't too sure if I should ask.

"Thanks for coming today, you know."

She made a 'hmm' noise and started typing back pretty quietly, seemingly to be having an argument via text with someone. It was hard for me not to ask her what was up as I hated seeing her in any way upset.

"Honestly though, it's nice that we can maybe spend some time together. I know you don't think I've changed, but I really have Kim. I'm not that same guy from high school."

I was rambling as I took the BC-99 from Cleveland Ave. Trying to stop myself, I waited for her to reply, but she seemed too busy on her phone. Great, this was going to be a fun car ride. Turning up the radio a little as my playlist started belting out Ed Sheeran – "Fall". Wanting to sing along, I had to stop myself, I didn't want to annoy her any more.

Finally, after what felt like hours she tossed her phone into her handbag. Sighing deeply, she rubbed her forehead, and took a few deep breaths. Clearly a trick to maybe calm herself down. She looked just as beautiful as the day at the rink, in a pair of tight black leggings, black ankle boots and an orange sweater with dogs dressed up as ghosts.

"You alright?" I dared to ask.

She looked at me with an annoyed side eye then looked out the window, clearly contemplating if she should even answer me.

"My brother. I called him after I spoke to you and asked him about colors, and I mentioned that I was bringing a date to the wedding and he ignored me. So, while I was waiting for you I texted him asking if he had heard me."

She paused, and as I quickly glanced back at her I could see in the reflection of the window she was biting her bottom lip. Huh, so she still did that when she was anxious.

"I told him you were going to be my date and he's not impressed, but he's calmed down now and suggested we all go out to watch the school's football match next weekend. Clear the air."

"And are you alright with that?"

"Honestly, not really. Sam, you came here and managed to turn my little, small life upside down and I was just starting to get it back."

"I'm sorry for the poor timing."

That was all I could say, I didn't want her to see me as a bad guy or the enemy. I wanted to at least be friends again. Just as we were once, a lifetime ago. I knew she got married and I knew she was building her life, even when I didn't want to know. My mom insisted I knew what everyone was doing in town, more so after I stopped visiting.

"It's not your fault," she said looking back at me with a small attempt of a smile. "When Luke died last year, I didn't really want to do anything. The year was a blur, his last few days, and the funeral all mashed together. That day at the rink, it was my first day back and well, I didn't expect to see you."

Was this her opening up a little? I didn't want to press, I just wanted her to know I was listening as we continued on our way. The journey was going to take around forty-five minutes which would give us plenty of time to chat, or not chat, whatever she wanted.

"I would never have taken you as a Swiftie."

She surprised me as she turned up the volume as Taylor Swift – "Shake It Off" started to play. It made me chuckle a little as she had started to dance a little in her seat and mumbling some of the words.

"Why wouldn't I be? She's awesome."

Tapping the steering wheel as this song always made me a little happy, even when the world felt as if it was closing in.

"Look, any guy who says he doesn't like Taylor Swift is a liar."

Clapping my hands quickly, she laughed at my antics. I felt her take some of her bricks down on that very high wall she had built. Perhaps my plan of sticking us into a car together was working.

"Can I ask," turning the volume down as the song ended and I bit my tongue wondering if I should even ask.

"How did Luke die?"

I waited, thinking she was going to tell me to piss off and we would have to turn the car around. I knew I had just changed the whole tone for the ride as we had just been dancing moments ago, but I had been wanting to ask for a while now.

"He had a Cardiac Sarcoma," she paused looking out the window again, "It's a rare type of tumor in the heart. And would you believe it, that's not what killed him." She laughed awkwardly, as if she had gone through this entire conversation before.

"He had the surgery and they removed it, it was benign, but then he bled out on the table... They couldn't get him back."

She said it as if it had just happened, her voice filled with sorrow, and I knew she was trying desperately not to cry. I kicked myself for asking as I had now ruined what would have been perhaps a nice day.

"I did get a chance to say goodbye though before they took

him up to surgery. There was a chance he wouldn't make it as the tumor was sitting in one of the chambers of his heart. My parents and my brother's fiancée sat with me in the waiting room, it was nearly ten hours later when the doctors came in. But I already knew. I felt it minutes before they came upstairs to find us."

She stopped again and if I was able to pull over, I would have and given her a hug, but the highway had no bays, and I didn't think she'd actually want a hug. How was I going to lighten the mood. I had no idea.

"You know, I always feel sorry for the doctors when they have to say they did everything they could, and the relatives get angry. I knew they tried everything, it's their job to do no harm and to protect life, but as my mom put it, God decided he needed Luke back and so he collected him."

"Fuck God!"

I shouted, not realizing my thoughts had been said out loud and she looked at me surprised.

"Sorry, I know your family are believers, but I can't believe in something, or someone, that willingly takes loved ones away."

She huffed a laugh, and I wasn't sure if it was because of my outburst or if she was feeling uncomfortable. A conversation about religion wasn't one anyone really enjoyed, unless it was with other people who believed as you did.

"It's alright, you are allowed to believe what you choose to. I believe God did take him and he's no longer in pain. Those last weeks with him were hard and I knew he tried so desperately to hold on, hold on for me. I'm very lucky I got to spend the time I did with him."

I wanted to shout at her a little then, as it didn't seem fair when she deserved more time with her husband. He meant so much to her, I could see it as she spoke of him, how it broke her up inside. And even if she despised me and was only putting up with me for the time being, I still wanted her to feel that she could talk to me.

"I am sorry you lost him, Kim. I'm sure he was a great guy, and you don't deserve this pain."

"He was a wonderful man."

"Maybe you can tell me about him sometime."

"Yeah, maybe sometime."

The car ride was pretty silent from there on. I hated how I had destroyed a pretty chilled ride by asking such a morbid and unhappy question. I had my fingers and toes crossed for when we arrived at Caulfeild, hoping the atmosphere and the change of scenery would help. Knowing I had to keep my head down as well was going to be tough. I was sure there would be some sort of paparazzi hiding behind a bush of some kind if the shop had given word to the media I was coming.

CHAPTER 8
Kimberly

O nce we passed the sign for Caulfeild, I felt the tension in my shoulders relax slightly. We had been quiet for the last ten minutes and of course, it was my doing. Sharing how Luke died hurt my heart, but I had a feeling Sam would eventually ask me. I didn't think so soon into our journey, but part of me didn't mind telling him.

"So, my brother told me he and Beth have decided on Christmas colors, reds, golds, greens, etc." I finally spoke, breaking the silence.

Trying to finally change the subject, I knew Sam wouldn't have been able to really say anything after my last words. Luke was a wonderful man and truly he would take my breath away with everything he did. Eventually I would be able to start talking about him again and not his illness.

"Oh, cool, the shop should have something I'm sure, that would fit that theme as well as something for you, maybe."

"I think we may only end up shopping for you."

"You never know, you might see something you like."

Smiling that awkward smile you do when you pass a stranger in the street, I was grateful when we pulled into an undercover car park. Once pulled into a space, Sam leaned into the back seat and pulled out a baseball cap and a normal black leather jacket.

"Ideally, I'd like not to be spotted today."

He had noticed me watching him intently and it clicked then. I was sitting next to the captain of one of the best hockey teams in Canada and currently, he was on a break hiding away in our small town. If word got out where he was, there was no telling what the news outlets would do. If the shop had been notified he was coming, that may have meant the media would know, too.

"I just don't want today being spoiled by a stupid amount of cameras."

"Hey, I'm not judging, you gotta do what you gotta do."

As he got out, I noticed how tidy he looked and here I was in a pair of black leggings and looking as unkempt as ever. If I had known he was going to 'steal' me today, I would have at least done my hair and stuck on some makeup and not looked like some character out of a Halloween movie.

Opening the passenger door for me, he held his hand out and I happily took it. I wasn't used to this gentleman side of him, even Luke would very rarely open a car door for me, so this was a new experience altogether.

"I checked the map before I left, the shop is just a block from here."

"Lead the way."

As we exited the car park, I took in the busy high street. It was decorated with beautiful harvest and autumn decorations. Walking along the street, I spotted maintenance men up on ladders, leaning against street lamps hooking up what looked like Christmas lights. They were getting ready for the festivities it seemed.

No one batted an eyelid as we walked together, crossing

the street and heading down another, passing a diner filled with happy voices. Sam looked back occasionally to see if I was still following him and although I was getting distracted by my surroundings, I tried to keep up and finally we reached the Henry Rosen store. Just by the look on the outside, I knew it was an expensive upper end boutique.

The door was unlocked and opened for us, with a stunning sales assistant standing in most likely her finest dress, waiting for us. Her blonde hair was up in a neat bun with a black ribbon tied around it, her eyes lit up as she spotted Sam then lowered to me, looking me up and down before gesturing us to come in.

"It's so wonderful to see you, Mr. Jones, my name is Izabella, please come in, welcome to *Henry Rosen*. My colleagues and I have set up a space for you and your assistant with many options."

"Oh, this is Kimberly and she's not my assistant, she's my date."

Date?! This was in no way a date! We were just here to look for a suit and possibly a dress, that was it. Even with the wedding coming up, he wasn't really my date then either. Izabella looked at me a little shocked then composed herself, smiling that salesperson smile and locked the door behind us.

"Right this way then, please."

As she started to walk in front of us, I pulled Sam back and looked at him with surprise and anger in my eyes.

"Date? This is not a date."

"I thought we were, you know, 'fake dating'?" Holding his fingers up to make quotation marks, then he took my hand, smiling.

"Would you rather me tell her you are my assistant and have her try to hit on me in front of you?"

"She can flirt with you all she wants."

"Yes, but then that would be rude to you, when I am here with you."

He smiled an even brighter smile then, squeezing my hand a little. How could I resist that smile? Allowing him to lead me, we followed Izabella up a set of stairs and into an open planned space filled with ball gowns and formal wear.

"Your team expressed you also wanted to look at dresses, I understand now why. Are you going to match for the occasion?"

"Yes, I think that would be best."

"Wonderful! Ok, Mr. Jones, if you can just sit here, I will take Kimberly to look at some dresses and we can then hopefully pick one and match your suit to compliment her dress."

"That sounds perfect, thank you, Izabella."

I could have kicked him there and then. He was really enjoying this whole fake dating thing already and we hadn't even been to the event where we needed to somewhat pretend! He was exhausting, but still seemed to be his playful self, the fun guy I fell in love with back in high school. Yet, I was nervous and continued to wait for the other shoe to drop and for him to disappoint me once again.

Izabella led me into a rather large changing room, a bit too large for one single person, but I tried not to question it. This seemed to be a very expensive shop and I hoped I didn't find a dress I loved and couldn't afford.

"If you can get undressed down to your underwear, I can go pull a few dresses. Is there any style you'd like to see?"

She asked as she leaned against the door frame, and I felt very exposed. The underwear I had on was no way near 'date' acceptable and the bra was one of those ugly comfy ones you threw on when you just needed to keep the girls strapped in.

"Eh – I'm my brother's best man, so I guess something

wedding appropriate, maybe full length? Dark green would be good."

"I will see what I can find."

She left then, shutting the door behind her and I stood in the middle of the room on the small round stool surrounded by mirrors. I could see every angle of my body once I stripped. Crystal may have been right with the fact I had lost weight this past year. My toned body from figure skating was slowly disappearing, perhaps I did need to eat more than one meal a day.

Soon Izabella reappeared holding three or four dresses, all different styles and different shades of green in her arms. Hanging them up one by one on a rail hooked on one of the walls, she looked at me and already I knew she was questioning what she had to work with.

"Right! Well, I thought as you are quite slim, we could try an A-Line first with a swooped illusion neckline. It has these cute ruffled capped sleeves as well."

Pulling out a pine-colored dress, she pulled it gently over my head. I looked at it for a few seconds and instantly regretted it. The style gave me no shape and just fell flat. I could see over my shoulder Izabella felt the same as she pulled a slightly disgusted face.

"Ok, no, definitely not! This just looks like a sack of potatoes on you."

Unzipping it and almost throwing it onto a small arm chair across the changing room, she then grabbed the next dress. This time it was in a peacock green shade, with spaghetti straps, a cowl neckline, and a V-shaped back.

"This one is better, but I don't like this shape on you. It does nothing for you. Hang on, I have an idea."

Leaving me standing in the second dress, she left the room. While she was gone I eyed the remaining two dresses she had left hanging up, all similar in style as the previous two.

She returned holding the dress over her shoulder, trying to clearly hide it from me. Smiling a little, I turned away so she could hang it up and then unzip me from the dress she'd left me in.

"Now, I know you said green, but Mr. Jones just mentioned this is for a Christmas themed wedding. We aren't meant to be showing this collection till next week, but I have this feeling that this might be the perfect dress."

Lifting the dress off the hanger then slowly she slipped it over my head. The soft feather-like fabric brushed against my skin as it fell into place. Izabella stood in front of me, blocking my view in the mirror, and adjusted the sleeves then pulled the dress down to sit perfectly on my hips before taking my hair out of its bun and shaking it a little over my shoulders, then she stepped out of my view.

I couldn't quite comprehend that I was looking at myself in the mirror, this dreamy, romantic, velvet, dark red dress fitted my body perfectly, giving off ethereal vibes. It hung just off-the-shoulder with capped sleeves resting just below my shoulders and the neckline cut into a sweetheart. Looking down, I saw the slit run up just above my knee and although it looked a little revealing, I was already in love.

"It also has pockets and what girl doesn't love a dress with pockets," Izabella commented as she stood beside me. "Now this, this is the dress. Shall we go show Mr. Jones?"

"Oh um – Sure, only thing it's a little long."

"Nothing a pair of heels won't fix, what size shoe are you? I will go grab you a pair now."

"Eh, five."

Off she disappeared for hopefully the last time, then returned holding a pair of black Jimmy Choo pumps in suede. I didn't dare ask for the price of anything as I knew there was no way I could afford any of it. I had originally thought I'd head to the local dress shop in town or look online for a second-hand dress that would work. Instead, here I stood in an expensive store wearing a dress that felt like magic.

Heading back towards Sam, who was sitting in the waiting area drinking a cup of coffee and stuffing his face with cookies, I felt nervous and a bit sick. I couldn't help but wonder if this was over doing it. I didn't want to upstage the bride.

"Wow. Holy crap, Kimmy!"

He sat there, shock written all over his face and I felt a blush rush to my cheeks. The last time anyone looked at me like that was Luke. I had to lower my eyes feeling some second-hand embarrassment.

"Izabella, look at her. Yep, that's the one, right?"

He stood up taking me all in as I stood on the floor stool and stared at myself in the mirror. I felt worried then that Bethan wouldn't be too happy with me and wondered if I should send her a photograph as I was sure she mentioned her sisters were going to be her bridesmaids and maybe we should all match.

"I don't know, Sam, it's a beautiful dress, but Bethan, my brother's fiancée might get upset. I don't even know what the bridesmaids are wearing."

"Sorry, but aren't you your brother's best man?" He stood next to me looking at me in the mirror.

"Yes."

"Then if you're worried, call your brother and see what he thinks, but honestly, we aren't leaving this store without this dress."

"I can't afford something like this."

"Don't you worry about that. Call your brother." Turning

away from me with a smile on his face, he looked at Izabella who seemed extra pleased with herself.

"Iz, let's go find me a suit to match Kim while she gets on the phone."

Off they went and I looked at myself in the mirror once again, still shocked that it was me looking back. The last time I was this dressed up was to judge an ice-skating contest and back then, Luke was my date.

Heading back to the changing room, I took my phone from my handbag and snapped a few pictures in the mirror before sending them over to my brother asking what he thought as well as to my mother.

Straight away my mother started to video call me and I let it ring for a second or two before answering it and her face said it all, jaw dropped to the floor with tears in her eyes.

"Please tell me you are not leaving that store without that dress! And anyway, where are you?"

Shit. I didn't think about where I was or who I was with, it was automatic to text my mom if I had an outfit in mind for something and needed her opinion. Already Joe was annoyed with me about my choice of date and I was surprised he hadn't already mentioned it to mom. Which meant I was now going to drop the ball.

"Would you be mad if I said I was in Caulfeild with umm," I paused, biting my bottom lip and mom's eyes narrowed on the screen.

"Kimberly Morgan, who are you with?"

"Ummm, Samuel Jones."

Her shouting was untranslatable, and I had to quickly turn down the volume of my phone. She was pissed and I felt a rush of disappointment flood my body. I hated making my mom mad, but this was slightly unavoidable now, she would have found out eventually.

"DO YOU NOT REMEMBER THE HELL HE PUT YOU
AND YOUR BROTHER THROUGH!? FOR YEARS!! AND,
THEN HE DUMPED YOU THE NIGHT OF PROM!! AND
YOU ARE NOW IN A SHOP WITH HIM?!"

There it was, the ball had dropped. Sam had always
bullied Joseph in high school, along with Crystal's younger
brother Jamie. I hated myself so much back then when I
started to have feelings for him. I was meant to be the angry
big sister who protected her brother. But when I was ordered
to tutor him, even Crystal, although mad at me, understood it
was something I had to do for school.

"Mom, please stop yelling. It's not like that."

"Then what is it Kimberly? What exactly is this?"

I went to speak, but something was stopping me, was it a
concern? Worry that she was going to yell some more, put the
phone down and not speak to me? My mom had a tendency to
give the silent treatment when she was mad and although it
was infuriating it was just her way of working through things.

"He's just my date to the wedding, okay. The girls thought
since the whole prom thing he had to make it up to me."

Silence.

"Your father wants you to bring him round for dinner and,
THEN we will decide if he will be your date."

As she hung up the phone, I looked back at myself in the
mirror. Tears were trying desperately to escape from my eyes
and my semi-good mood had now disappeared.

Following Izabella through the many, many rails of suits, all different shades, colors, and fabrics. She pulled some out and held the few up against me and then would shake her head and put them back on the rail. She was obviously looking for something and I guessed it was different with guys. Girls wanted to try on all the dresses they could find and twirl and spin while wearing them. I only knew that because of my sister.

After her and mom would come back from a clothing shopping spree, mostly thrift shops. Mom would have Jane try every single item on and parade around in front of dad and me. They were mostly the most basic of clothes, but sometimes Jane would get her way. When that happened, mom would buy her a big poofy dresses she could pretend to be a princess in.

Feeling a lump forming in my throat as I thought about Jane, I shook my head and banished those thoughts to the back of my mind. I was here with Kim, and I was going to make sure we enjoyed ourselves today.

"Ah, how about this one?"

Holding a deep red velvet tuxedo against me, Izabella's smile widened as she rushed off to grab what I guessed were a pair of shoes and I headed back to the waiting room to find Kimberly. She was sitting there back in her normal clothes, but still with her hair down.

"How was your phone call?"

"Not how I thought it would go, my mom phoned me once I sent over the photos to Joe. She asked me where I was and who I was with. I half expected Joe to have already told her I was having you as my date. But she didn't seem at all impressed, there was a lot of shouting."

Her eyes dropped to the floor as she fiddled with the hem of her sweater. I wanted to take hold of her hands then, tell her everything was okay, but forced myself to stay put. Running my fingers through the front of my hair, I sighed and sat down, wondering what I was meant to say. She'd had an argument because of me, because I was here.

"They want you to come to dinner, as I expected."

"Sounds good, I will be happy to."

"I know you mean well, and I appreciate that, but can you just take me home."

Disappointment immediately set in with her request. I was hoping she'd let me take her out for lunch or an early dinner after this, but alas respecting Kim's wishes would come first.

"Ok, Mr. Jones, I've got your measurements here, would you like to try on the suit?"

Izabella came back in with the same happy smile on her face and held both the suit and shoes in her hands. When she finally looked at Kimberly then to me, her smile dropped a little.

"Thank you, Izabella, but actually Kimberly isn't feeling too hot, so I'm going to take her home. If you can ring up both outfits including any extras we may need, please."

Pulling out my wallet then credit card, I handed it over to her without a second thought. Kim's eyes shot up as Izabella disappeared with my card.

"You can't buy me that dress!" she shouted.

"I can buy whatever I like actually," I joked, and she didn't seem impressed with me. "I owe it to you and anyways, you are not leaving without that dress, it would be a shame. So tough, I am buying it and it will be sent to you when it's ready."

She didn't protest or continue to get mad, she just scowled at me, and I couldn't help but smile. Although many years had passed between us, she still had the same mannerisms and tells. It was cute, she was still cute – Beautiful even.

"There you go, Mr Jones; I will have our tailors and seamstresses sort out both garments for you and they will be sent to the address your assistant gave us."

Once we were done and said our thank yous, Kim followed me out of the store and into the main street again. Some of the streetlamps had been switched on as the fall sun was starting to set and it looked like a whole different place.

Christmas twinkle lights trailed lamp post to lamp post. Each shop window had some form of fall, harvest or Christmas display already going up. There was an evening styled farmers market set up across the street.

"Shall we go and grab a cup of coffee before we leave?"

Please say yes, please say yes.

Sighing, Kim rolled her eyes at me then smiled a little.

"Coffee sounds nice, but only one."

Inner me cheered as I felt a pinch of happiness, I didn't want to ruin this day. Although she wanted to go home, I was hoping it was just due to her argument with her mom and nothing to do with me.

"I just have to make a quick phone call; I need someone to go in and check on Daisy."

"Ah yeah, your dog. How old is she?"

"She will be six in January. I hate leaving her for this long, but I know Crystal will happily go over and check on her. She'll let her out and most likely spend the rest of the day there as I know she closes the café early on Sundays."

Giving her some privacy as she walked a few steps away from me to make her call, I pulled out my own phone. It looked like I had missed a few texts and at least ten phone calls from Paula, my personal assistant. I had put my phone on silent once I picked up Kimberly. I felt it would have been rude if my phone kept ringing or while I was trying to talk to her.

"WHERE THE HELL HAVE YOU BEEN?!"

"Hello, Paula, sorry my phone was on silent, what's up?"

"WHAT'S UP?! Don't you dare 'what's up' me for god's sake!"

Paula had been my personal assistant since I signed on with the Devils and back then I was just a sub. She had taken a chance on me and for that, I would always be grateful for her. When I spent my first Christmas alone, she was mortified and demanded I spend the next one with her and her family. Ever since then, I have spent every holiday season with her, her husband and their four kids. That was ten years ago. They were my second family now.

"Sorry, I just didn't want my phone blowing up while I was out with Kim."

"Look, I get that you want to make amends with this woman. I'm happy to see your growth, but do not, I repeat DO NOT sleep with her. You did not tell me this was Kimberly Morgan, the world champion figure skater! And you didn't tell me she was your high school sweetheart."

"Did I not?"

She was shouting, pissed and acting dumb was not going to bode well for me. If she was in front of me, she would have smacked the crap outta me. Oops.

"Don't play dumb with me, you shit!"

"Now, now, Paula, no need for name calling."

"Cram it! I have been looking after you for years. I got rid of all those women who wanted to steal your money, or make babies with you to claim checks. And now this?! You cannot screw this up!"

"You're making it sound like Kim is some sort of skating royalty. She won a few awards, but she's not retired."

I could hear the sigh on the other end of the phone, and I glanced at Kimberly as she continued her phone call. We were standing just off Main Street, hidden by a few buildings and the wind was already picking up as a chill went through my clothes. Kim hadn't *just* won a few awards. I had watched her shows and kept up with the news as best as I could throughout the years. When her husband became ill, she just stopped and disappeared. She had disappeared back home it seemed.

"Samuel, listen to me and I am only going to say this once. This woman has been through hell and back from what I have found out today. She was forced to retire, because her husband got sick then died. If you are just looking for some fling or a hookup, this isn't the one you want to do it with. Find someone else."

"Would it surprise you to know, this isn't just some random hook up? Kim and I have a history, there are things I want to try and repair with becoming friends as the end goal. Anything after that, well that's for her to decide."

Paula went silent on the other end of the phone, which was something I wasn't used to and worried me more. If I didn't hear her sigh, I would have sworn she had hung up on me. It wouldn't have been the first time either.

"Alright, but try to stay out of the public's eye. This would end in a PR disaster if it's not planned correctly."

She hung up then. Paula always meant well, and I knew deep down she did care about me. I wasn't just someone who paid her, we were friends, maybe even thought of me as family. When I turned around, feeling awful for my delay while on the phone, Kimberly was just looking idly into the windows of the closed shops.

"Sorry about that, my eh, personal assistant can be pretty demanding." Shrugging my shoulders, I popped my phone back in my pocket and joined her.

"That's alright, you're a busy guy – Now, how about that coffee."

My ears perked up when she mentioned coffee and for a moment, I had forgotten about it. I honestly thought she would return after her phone call and decide she wanted to go home instead, but obviously Crystal had convinced her to stay. I would have to thank her next time I saw her.

"When I found the suit shop, it said on the map there was a gin and coffee bar in the opposite street. Obviously, we don't have to have gin."

"I am partial to a glass of gin or two, however as you are driving it wouldn't be fair."

I struggled trying to keep my smile from beaming across my cheeks and possibly blinding her. I gestured for her to go first and turned down the street directly opposite the suit shop, we found the gin and coffee bar pretty much instantly.

Ginbeans & Co

A play on words, but a clever name. Kimberly stepped in first, with me following close behind. The bar was decorated with Christmas lights and tinsel already. It even had a

Christmas tree with coffee cup shaped ornaments decorating the far corner. Not as busy as I thought it would be, but still busy enough, so we didn't draw too much attention to ourselves.

I was crossing my fingers and toes no one recognized me, but then again, who was I kidding. This was Canada and hockey was pretty much our national sport.

Grabbing a booth in a corner tucked away slightly from view, but we could still see the front door. Kim tossed her small bag down on the seat next to her and I sat opposite her. Even in the slight glow of the fairy lights, she looked beautiful.

"So, why are you 'really' here then? Hiding away from the world and its cameras."

Her question took me by surprise. She looked at the menu then lifted her eyes to watch me, her eyelashes doing some sort of flutter, lifting in the corners. She was smiling a little.

"I, eh, I got into a fight with one of my teammates and well, they put me on leave for stress."

"Ah."

Her response was simple, and I waited with bated breath to see if she would say anything else. When the waitress came to our table, I lowered my head, a little out of her gaze. She first asked Kimberly what she'd like, a caramel latte large, then me. I hadn't even had a chance to look at the menu yet so I just picked something random off the menu and had no idea what it even was.

"Okay, so that's a large caramel latte with whipped cream and chocolate dust and for you, a gingerbread chocolate mocha with cream!"

The waitress seemed too happy and grinned a little like a Chester cat or like one of those creepy China dolls my grandma would keep in her house. Her eyes were wide and surrounded by black eyeliner. I only noticed as Jane would often wear her make up the same and that would creep me out even then.

"That sounds like a diabetic fit in drink form. You sure that's what you wanted?" Kimberly asked, appearing to hold back a laugh.

"Oh, it does, yeah. I don't know, I just picked something at random. Normally, I'd have ordered a black coffee with two sugars, but then I didn't want to come across as boring."

"Hmm, you continue to surprise me, Mr. Jones."

"I am full of surprises."

Winking at her, she shook her head smiling while a little blush hinted at her cheeks. Once the waitress came back with our drinks, we were left to sit there in content silence. I wasn't sure if I should continue our conversation about why I had been benched or if this was even an appropriate place to do it.

"So, aside from a big Swifie, any other secrets I should know about?"

"Oh, I also love Harry Styles, but that's more of a man crush type of thing. He's a nice guy, I've met him a couple of times at those award show things."

"You've met loads of celebrities then, I'm guessing."

"Didn't you? You know when you were in the games."

She lowered her eyes and stared at her drink before taking a sip. I hadn't been brave enough to taste mine yet. I wasn't looking forward to the massive sugar rush it would bring.

"You know, I don't really remember, that feels like a long time ago now. I stopped attending the games nearly three years ago. Once Luke became ill... I just stopped."

"Do you miss it?"

"Everyday."

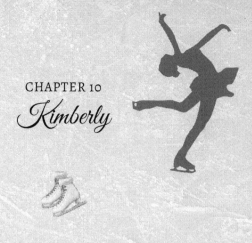

Sitting across a table from Samuel Jones was the last thing I thought my Sunday was going to become. Even with the dress and suit shopping, I did not foresee this and neither did my witchy friends. He had already smiled at me like a kid who got the last sweet after I agreed to join him for coffee. But now, he was bringing up my past. He sure knew how to pick awkward subjects.

I hadn't really forgotten what it was like being in that spotlight. But the life of a champion figure skater was short lived. The life on the ice in general was, unless you went off to do other things, such as coaching. I, still with a huge love for skating, wanted to teach.

Letting out a soft sigh, I try to bring myself back to the present. So, Sam had attacked another team player. He had mentioned aggression before, but I didn't think he meant physically. And so now he was 'on leave', I knew that was code for the bench until further notice. I didn't want to pry anymore out of him after that, I imagined he'd eventually tell me.

"How are your parents?"

Changing the subject as fast as I could, he drew back a little as if struck. I could see his thoughts as they played on his face.

"Eh – I wouldn't know, truth be told they don't know I'm back."

"Surely not? Sam! We live in a town filled with gossip mongers, I bet they do."

He swallowed hard and I wondered why he was keeping his arrival from his family. After all they had kept up with his career, I was sure.

"I didn't come back after Jane died, and I don't think my mom would want to see me, dad especially."

Wow, these conversations weren't going as well as I thought they would have. During the car journey, in the shop and now here, everything just seemed to stall or completely stop.

"Bloody hell," I uttered and he choked back a laugh. I had never been someone who cussed, but it seemed right to do so.

"So far, we've talked about dead husbands, missing my old job, you punching someone, and now you're not talking to your parents. Wow – When did our lives become so dark?"

"Pretty sure it was when we hit that big age of twenty-one and alcohol was introduced properly."

"Speaking of alcohol, does your coffee have a funny taste?"

He had finally started to drink his weird gingerbread coffee thing. Clearly he was enjoying it as half the glass was already empty and mine almost gone. Even with the funny taste, I wouldn't have minded ordering another one until it clicked. Gin and coffee bar. My eyes widened as I grabbed the menu and looked down to find our drinks. With a soft groan, I closed my eyes in frustration.

"Our drinks contain seven percent of alcohol from the gin. It's gin infused coffee."

Gulping back the last sip of his drink, Sam's face shared the same expression as me. We really didn't read the menu correctly. And now, he was most certainly over the limit for driving us home.

"Well, that's eh – interesting."

He shrugged and decided to laugh it off before calling the waitress back over.

"Does all your coffees come with gin in them?" He asked.

"Yep, they sure do! Well, no, actually, we have about three that are just plain old regular coffee. Would you like to order something else?"

"Sure, why not. Do you have a list of non-coffee gin drinks??"

"We do have a cocktail menu, yes; I shall go fetch it for you."

As the waitress rushed off, I wanted to smack Sam over the head with the menu board. What was he thinking? We didn't need more alcohol in us! Especially not me as I had already drunk a fair amount last night and I had work in the morning. I couldn't very well stay out in another city.

"What are you doing? We shouldn't be drinking more; we should get you a normal coffee and some food then we can head home."

"Sorry, no, I cannot do it; I don't drink and drive."

"You drove me home yesterday after having a beer!!"

"Nope, that was Becks Light, alcohol free. And besides, why don't we lighten up a little and enjoy this time without any responsibilities. Daisy is sorted and I'm sure what's her face down at the rink won't care either if you're late."

I felt myself sigh as part of me realized I would get the chance to spend the night with Sam. We may both loosen up a little after a few drinks down us. Perhaps I could finally find out what really happened prom night and why he never spoke to me again.

Once the waitress came back with the cocktail menu, I ordered for us both, a long island ice tea and a gin and tonic. He was right, why not? I hadn't had the chance to really loosen up or relax in months and oddly I felt perfectly safe with Sam.

An hour or so later, we had consumed many cocktails, several bowls of fries and a burger each. Both Sam and I were giddy and the café was slowly closing up shop. The sun was now lower in the sky as the evening was beginning to greet us. I felt an odd twinge in my stomach. I didn't want to leave.

"I'm sorry, we will be calling last orders shortly. I can grab you both a coffee to go if you'd like?"

"Will... What... AH!" slurring my words as I tried to pull a sentence together, Sam just laughed across the table. "Will it have gin?"

Eventually I got there after a few breaths and a hiccup or two.

"Yes, I can make you a special one."

"LOVELY!" I shouted, clapping my hands as Sam finished up his drink.

"None for me, thanks." He smiled as he passed the waitress a fifty-dollar bill and her eyes lit up at her tip.

"Can you tell me where the nearest and nicest hotel is?"

Why wasn't he slurring his words? I was sure he was drinking the same amount as me, but now as I looked at him, he had a glass of...maybe cola last? I wasn't sure.

"Oh, there's the *New Tree Hotel*, it's about five, maybe ten minutes' walk from here. Really nice place, it's a four star, I think." The waitress answered before rushing off.

"You're staring at me, again," he teased me.

"No – I," lowering my eyes, I finished my drink and waited patiently for our takeaway cups to arrive.

Huffing a laugh under his breath, Samuel hummed to the low sound of music in the background as I tried to look everywhere but him. It was just us here. There were three remaining staff. The waitress who was making our drinks, a busboy who was cleaning up the tables, and the manager who I believed was counting the till.

"Come on, let's go find this hotel then, shall we?"

Standing up and helping me put on my jacket, he shrugged his on lazily. The waitress met us at the front door with our coffees and once out, she locked it behind us. I knew I was tipsy, but as soon as the air hit my lungs, I felt an overwhelming sensation of the world spinning. Looping my arm into Sam's to help keep me up right and steady, he placed a warm hand over mine and smiled at me.

"How ...are you ...okay?" I managed to question as we began walking towards the hotel.

"Ah, those little drinks don't do much. I get drunk mostly on beer."

"Well, that's not okay!" I shouted again and Sam chuckled a little. "We MUST find a store... FAST! Right... now!"

"Okay, and why do we need to do that?"

"Snacks and... beer!"

He was choking back an even bigger laugh as I let go of his arm. I had started walking with determination, even though I had absolutely no idea where I was going. Catching up to me then, Sam wrapped an arm around my waist and pulled me back, spinning me in the process causing me to slam into his chest.

"Sor – Sorry."

"It's alright. Maybe we can order room service instead."

Pulling out his phone as he held me closely, one hand

started to idly rub my back. I was painfully aware of that one hand, even if it only gently touched on my lower back. Rocking a little back and forth, the floor beneath my feet was shaking a little. It didn't deter him as he kept hold of me and seemed to be looking at his sat nav.

"It's up this way. Come on."

Guiding me then, we walked what felt like forever in the brisk fall air. As we crossed a street or two, we went down a few pathways until we reached the hotel, and he never took his arm away from my waist.

Kim looked just as beautiful as she did the day we met. She walked into bio class and was told to sit next to me. The new girl.

The hotel only had two choices of rooms left as a wedding had booked out many of the rooms. One was a single occupant room and the other a double, family size.

Kimberly's eyes almost lit up when they mentioned the one double. I wasn't sure if it was my imagination, but she seemed slightly excited, or maybe it was just the drink that made me think otherwise.

"So, we will head up, freshen up and do you fancy going down to the bar for a few more drinks? The night is still young."

Please say yes, please say yes.

"Sure! But what are we freshening up for? Not like we have a change of clothes."

"Ah, that's very true. Alright, so bar now?"

She nodded with enthusiasm and headed off in the direction of the bar. Or was it the bar? I had no idea, but we followed the signs and directions. Passing the function room door, Kim couldn't help herself as she popped her head inside to see the happy newlyweds taking their first dance. I wasn't sure if I saw a hint of sadness on her face or tears of joy as she watched on.

"Come on. We aren't meant to be here."

Pulling her away, she looped her arm back into mine and I caught a whiff of her fading perfume, floral but subtle. She really could have worn a trash bag, and I still would have gone a little weak at the knees. She was stunning, and I hoped she knew that.

"Right, you sit there, and I will get us a drink or two."

"Or three!! Or a pitcher!!"

She raised her voice over the faint music and a few of the guests stared at her and rolled their eyes. I was hoping no one watched any hockey or at least didn't recognize me while we were here.

"What can I get ya?"

The bartender looked like he belonged in the wedding judging by how smartly dressed he was.

"Eh, your best beer on tap and for my lady friend, a strawberry daiquiri."

"Righto!"

Off the bartender went and I tried to keep my eye on Kimberly as she fiddled with the menus and tapped her feet. She would do that when we would go out for food. Always in another part of town so no one would see us together. Lowering my eyes, the shame of it all fell over me. I was never ashamed of being with her. I just knew if some of my friends saw I was with her, we would have got grief. They would have ensured I had treated her poorly in front of everyone.

But then again, I didn't treat her very well even when we were in school, and no one was watching us. I was such an asshole back then, no wonder she was apprehensive to really be around me, maybe she was just being polite now.

"Here you go, shall I open a tab for you, sir?"

"Eh, no that's alright. Thank you."

Heading back to the table after paying in cash again, I noticed Kim had quietened down. I hoped her mood hadn't shifted or she regretted this. Sipping her drink slowly, she smiled behind her straw as she began swaying a little to the music that played just down the hall in the function room.

"Shame we left those outfits at the shop, we could have snuck into that wedding and pretended to be guests of the couple. Distant cousins or something."

"Or I'm the filthy mistress of the bride's father and here to proclaim my love and our unborn child."

"You've clearly been watching too many dramatized Netflix shows."

She laughed and I couldn't help but join in with her. I could listen to her laugh every day if she'd let me. But then she suddenly settled and lowered her eyes, looking down at her drink then began rubbing her left hand, her ring finger. Her wedding ring is no longer there.

"Alright?"

Reaching across the table, I held my hand out hoping she might notice and take it, but instead she wrapped her hands around her glass.

"Yes, of course. Ha ha!"

Silent again and that weird sense of awkwardness hung in the air. I was hoping we'd be able to hang out some more, but now, she was slowly going quiet. She wasn't drinking and I couldn't really blame her, the bar was flat and had no real atmosphere.

"Shall we head up after this and order room service?"

"Sure, sounds good." She nodded happily.

"Are you sure you are okay?"

"Yeah, I'm fine, just a little dizzy that's all."

I was starting to feel like an ass. I could have easily phoned Paula and ordered a driver to come pick us both up, or at least pick Kimberly up and take her home. I got lost in the moment of perhaps spending more time with her and not letting the day end early. It was selfish of me.

"Kim, I can call you a driver if you want to be taken home? It's not a problem."

She sat for a few minutes as if deciding what she wanted to do. I wouldn't have blamed her if she decided she'd rather head home to sleep in her own bed. Suddenly, she tossed the straw out from her drink onto the table and began downing it. It was obvious she instantly regretted it as she held her forehead. "Screw that! We need to have some fun."

Once her brain freeze was over, she looked at me and then at my drink. Smiling a little she began clapping and smacking the table lightly.

"We like to drink with Sammy..."

She began singing and of course, made me laugh in return. Under her watchful glaze, I did as I was being ordered and downed my beer. Hoping I wouldn't bring any of it back up as it made me feel a little queasy.

"Let's get out of here. Sitting at a bar is for old guys."

Standing up, she reached over and pulled my hand, yanking me up and out of my seat. Heading out the door and down the long corridor again towards the hotel reception desk then through a side door towards a set of stairs. Still pulling me lightly, we raced up the stairs and for a moment I had no idea what she was up to. Until she let go of my hand and started raiding through a cleaning cart that had been left in the hallway.

Grabbing spare towels and throwing them at me, she was

giggling drunkenly to herself. She then began putting mini toiletries into her pockets and stuffing them in mine before fishing out the room key. Room 306. Smiling sweetly, she raced towards the elevator door and pressed the button to open, and I followed her sheepishly. I would have followed her anywhere at this point.

"Where to next?"

"Well, ideally, we need to get a fresh change of clothes. Could you maybe use that magic phone of yours and get something sent to us or would that be too rude and eh, late?"

"It is never too late for Paula."

"Great! Because I have an idea."

"Oh, more than stealing hotel freebies?"

"Hey! You can never have enough of the fancy soaps and stuff."

Winking at me as the doors opened to our floor, she raced off in front of me. Looking at every door until she finally found ours, she held the room key up to open it. Once inside, she switched on the lights and gasped a little under her breath.

I assumed she was used to top quality hotels after traveling around the globe for her competitions. But she still looked just as excited as a kid would on their first big summer vacation. I quietly watched her sit the towels and things onto a table that overlooked the landscape of the city. She wandered around the room looking through every draw and every cupboard.

Pulling my phone out, I hunted for Paula's number and decided it would be best to text her as phoning, she could become rather nasty and already this was going to open a can of worms.

Paula, can you get some clothes delivered to the New Tree Hotel.

And why do we need clothes, Samuel?

I may have had too much to drink and can't drive so I opted for the safest route to book a hotel room.

Is Kimberly still with you? I hope you are not going to do what I think you're going to do!

We have barely held hands. I'm not a player.

No, you're just a heartbreaker. But fine, I will get some clothes delivered to you in the next hour. Just behave please, we can't be dealing with more bad publicity.'

Smiling as I felt satisfied, after all I had not caused Paula some sort of heart attack. I looked over at Kimberly who had begun raiding the mini fridge. This bill was definitely going to cost me in the morning, but if she was happy and enjoying herself, I didn't care.

"Give or take, new clothes will be here shortly. Now can you tell me this idea of yours?"

"Make sure we get dress clothes. And maybe pajamas – Oh! And clean underwear! – Oh and maybe some socks."

"Anything else you'd like to add?"

I joked as she downed a mini bottle of gin. She was going on a 'let's mix my drinks mood' and I was sure she'd pay for it in the morning. Sending off another text to Paula about our requests, she responded with an angry face and a middle finger emoji. Luckily, I knew that usually meant she'd still do as I requested. Hopefully.

"So, dress clothes? Are you planning on sneaking us into that wedding then?"

"Hey! It will be fun, and we only live once, right?"

"Alright, but if we get caught, it was your idea."

"Deal!"

Chucking me over a mini bottle of vodka then, she gave me that same look as she did downstairs. Opening the bottle, it was just one gulp, a shot worth really. The liquid burnt as it went down, already I was beginning to feel the buzz.

CHAPTER 12
Kimberly

I shouldn't have been drinking as much as I was. I knew I had to keep my wits about me. I didn't think Sam would try anything with me, he seemed to be a gentleman. But it had been a very long time since I had been in a room, alone, with a man that wasn't my husband. And as much as I hated to think about it, a woman had needs and Sam was just as equally handsome as he was in his teens, if not more so in a rough and rugged way.

Watching as he took a seat on the edge of the bed and fiddled with the plastic mini bottle of vodka, he looked as nervous as I felt. That's why I needed liquid courage. Even if we had been in a room together previously, that time felt like another life. A lifetime ago.

Finally, after almost an hour and some scrolling through my phone, there was a knock on the door. Sam opened it and in popped a girl who couldn't be much taller than five feet. She seemed bouncy and way too eager, as her smile beamed across her face. Short black hair swished as she looked at me up and down, her blue eyes seeming to judge, but the smile never disappeared.

"Here you go, Mr. Jones. A suit and a dress for your companion."

She handed him a long dress bag and Sam hung it up against the bathroom door frame then she handed him a duffle bag, which I guessed was filled with a change of clothes and other things.

"Thank you, Emily, sorry to pull you away from the, eh – whatever it was you were doing."

"No probs, boss, Paula sends her regards and also told me to mention the image." She winked at him before again looking at me with a smile then leaving the room.

She was in and out in a flash, barely giving me a look. What did she mean by the image? Was that a codeword of some kind?

Getting up, I unzipped the dress bag and in front of Sam's grey suit was a navy-blue dress, drop shoulders and knee length. Pretty and would work nicely for our little wedding gate crashing plan.

"She also packed shoes and umm these?"

Looking over my shoulder, he was holding up a pair of black heels, a pair of black laced panties and a matching black bra. I could see the toying and playfulness in Sam's eyes as I snatched them out of his hands and headed into the bathroom, pushing the door shut.

Undressing and taking a good look at myself in the mirror, my hair was still down after the dress shop and I wasn't too sure how I was going to fix it up.

"Eh Kim, there were these in the bag as well."

Sam's hand poked round the door, holding some kind of toiletry bag. It made me laugh a little as he held it out, as if it were something diseased. Opening the bag, not only was there a brand-new hairbrush, but there was also brand-new make-up and moisturizer. His assistant really thought of everything.

Once I changed into some clean underwear, I put on a splash of makeup. I attempted to do the dress up, with no such luck as it was a zip up all the way on the back. Which now meant, Sam would have to help me.

Breathing in deeply as my nerves began to get the best of me, I looked at myself in the large bathroom mirror and tried to calm myself down, counting to ten.

"Sam, could you come and help me, please?"

He didn't reply at first and as the painful seconds went by, I wondered if he didn't hear me. Before I could call out to him again, he knocked on the bathroom door then slowly pushed the door open. Stepping inside, he was looking at me with a stunned look on his face.

"What, eh, can I help with?"

"Can you zip me up, please?"

"Oh, umm yeah sure, no problem."

Coming up behind me, I caught a glimpse of him in the mirror as he stood there. Both of us seemed to tremble a little. As he began to zip me up, I became incredibly hot and although he wasn't really touching me, I deeply wished he was.

Our eyes met in the mirror as his hand trailed up to move my hair over my shoulder then he finished zipping me up.

"It's a bit tough."

I didn't have anything to say. If I allowed my mouth to utter the words that were running through my mind, I would have come undone there and then. He cleared his throat before stepping back. Lowering my eyes from his gaze, I turned and picked up one of the black heels and slipped my foot in. Before I could put the other shoe on, he knelt and lifted my ankle to place the shoe on.

His warm hand wrapped around my skin and such a simple thing sent shivers up my thigh and a heat rose deep within me. A heat I had forgotten about. But within seconds, he was back up standing in front of me, a half-smile across his face as he licked his lips before turning away and walking back into the bedroom.

I wanted to scream and shout at that moment, and pounce him all at the same time. Bracing myself against the sink counter, I took a few deep breaths to calm myself down and compose myself.

"Are we doing this or not?"

Standing in the bathroom doorway, he looked at me as if I were his dessert. Even as he pulled his suit jacket on and held out his hand to me, he didn't take his eyes off me. He knew what he was doing, of course he knew. He was one of the biggest fuck boys in the entire hockey community and therefore, he knew all the moves.

Standing up straight and relaxing my shoulders, I wasn't going to let his smooth moves do anything to me. Or at least, I wouldn't let him know they affected me. We were going to sneak into that wedding, have a dance, grab a drink and heck maybe even do a fake speech! But what we weren't doing, was making googly eyes at each other, and taking each other's clothes off. Even if deep down, I really wanted to.

WE STOOD outside the main function room door as the music continued to blast and most of the guests were very, very drunk by this point. It was perfect timing for us as no one would even notice us just gate crashing. Well, unless the couple were sober and if they were, we'd be screwed and possibly thrown out of the hotel.

"Are you sure about this?"

Sam whispered in my ear as he came up behind me, sending more shivers down my spine and making me jump a little. I was getting cold feet myself and thinking that this was a stupid idea, and we should just head back to the bar.

"I'm, eh – maybe – I don't know."

"Problem is though Kim, if they recognize me."

"Oh shit, I didn't think of that."

I hadn't. It wasn't something that even came up while I was thinking of this fun silly plan. If he was spotted, the media would catch wind and his photographs would be all over the sports news. Yes, maybe this was a bad idea.

"Actually – Fuck it. We only live once right."

Without even a second's hesitation, Sam linked his fingers with mine. Pushing open the door, he pulled me inside as music blasted and hit my ears instantly.

The room was decorated beautifully for a wedding day. Shades of lilacs, pinks and sage greens were everywhere. The bridesmaids dressed in off the shoulder sage green dresses. The center pieces were tall crystal vases with ostrich feathers all dyed in the colors to match. Disco balls lit up the dance floor and beautiful fairy lights lit up the ceiling with drapes of satin white curtains.

It was absolutely gorgeous and gave me ideas for Joe's wedding. We could still stick to the Christmas theme, but fairy lights were a must have decoration.

Pulling me further in towards the bar, there was a large cocktail pitcher set up with a help yourself sign. After pouring two glasses, we turned to watch as everyone enjoyed themselves. I wondered how long it would take until we were spotted.

"You wanna dance?"

Sam leaned forward and shouted a little over the blaring

music as the dance floor filled with the sway of people. I had absolutely no idea what song the DJ was even playing as I had never heard it in my life. Some dance remix number and there was no way I was going to be able to dance to it.

"Maybe the next one."

I awkwardly took a sip of my drink. I saw Sam roll his eyes with an up to no good smile, before leaving me and heading towards the DJ. Oh God, he was going to request something wasn't he? After a few minutes of watching them, both of them were laughing and smiling together, he started walking back to me.

"I have a request tonight, from a very special VIP guest, who wishes to send their congratulations to the happy couple."

Shrugging off his jacket, he then held out his hand to me, Sam smiled at me and his eyes lit up. The song started to play, and I threw my head back laughing. Of course, he would pick Olly Murs, 'Dance with me Tonight'. He remembered my obsession over this guy through my teens and knew without fail, I'd get up and dance.

Taking his hand, he pulled me into a spring as we made our way to the dance floor swinging, side stepping, jigging, and jiving with it, whatever dance moves we could make together. We didn't seem that uncoordinated which was interesting. And as the song came to an end, it slowly faded into a slower song. Without a word, Sam pulled me into a slow dance to Eric Clapton, 'Wonderful Tonight'.

Some of the wedding guests left the dance floor, leaving it for the few couples that were left to dance together. Including the bride and groom, who slowly made their way to dance beside us. The groom's eyes lit up as he recognized Samuel.

"You're – You're - oh my god!!"

He shouted as he looked Sam up and down, gobsmacked.

His bride didn't seem to fully understand what was happening, other than noticing we were two gatecrashers of her wedding. If I were a bride, I may have been pissed.

"Honey, it's…"

The groom leaned towards his bride, whispering in her ear and her eyes lit up as she realized, looking back at Sam and me.

"I hope you don't mind us sneaking in." Sam leaned forward so they could hear him. "The bar was pretty boring."

"No, of course not, ha ha! You are welcome to stay!"

The groom was overly excited and seemed to be enjoying himself more now that a celebrity had joined his party. The groom wanted to continue some sort of conversation, but his bride smiled and whisked him away to continue their slow dance.

"I thought we were goners then, thankfully you're a famous hockey player, huh?" Winking at Sam, his face flashed a hint of red as he spun me out then pulled me back in.

"Where did you learn to dance?" I asked.

"I dated a girl back in college who was obsessed with period dramas. She made me take lessons with her; they've come in handy I think."

I felt a sudden tightness in my stomach as I thought about him with another girl. It was strange. I had read multiple news articles where he had been seen with different women, sometimes a different one each week. I knew he was that type of guy, or was he still one? I deeply hoped not.

"What happened?" He asked, leaning in towards me.

"Nothing. Why?"

"Your face dropped a little, was it something I said?"

Had my face given away my thoughts? I was pretty good at keeping a poker face on, I had to be. But then again, this was the most relaxed I had been in a long time. Dancing and enjoying myself, I was afraid when the other shoe was going to drop and how badly I'd feel it.

"In this room filled with people, you're the only woman I see right now," he whispered in my ear and my cheeks flushed red.

Looking up at him as his eyes darkened a little and a small smile appeared across his face, I felt that same heat running up my thighs. His voice was tender, and his eyes were filled with wanting. This wasn't supposed to happen. I was meant to avoid him as much as I could at the rink and yet, he kept showing up in the same places I was. And deep down, I didn't mind.

Letting go of him as the song stopped, I left him on the dance floor and headed back to the bar. I needed some air. Luke's face flashed in my mind as the memory of him came flooding back. What was I doing?

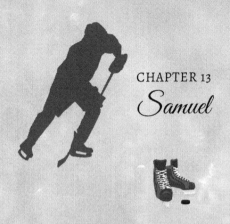

CHAPTER 13
Samuel

I watched Kim as she walked towards the bar then she suddenly turned to hurry out of the room. I grabbed my jacket but hestitated.. I wasn't sure if I should run after her, as my words must have offended her somehow.

Standing there a second or two, I realized there was no chance I'd let her walk out of this building without me.

Rushing out the door after her, I followed her into the lobby and watched her step outside. Maybe giving her a minute would be the best idea and I contemplated what I was going to do next. Apologize that was damn sure, I had clearly overstepped the mark, but the night just got me carried away.

Once the minute was up, I raced outside spotting her sitting on a bench just outside the hotel with her head in her hands. Shit, was she crying? I hoped not. I had already ruined our car ride here, and she wanted to go home after the shop. I had really fucked it now, hadn't I?

"Kimberly, I'm sorry, I should have kept my mouth shut."

I stood in front of her, a few steps away to still give her space she needed. She lifted her head up looking at me with her beautiful brown eyes. God, she was breathtaking.

"It's not you. Sam, if anything you've been the perfect gentlemen, it's me."

Lowering her eyes again, she started to fidget with the fabric of her skirt. I didn't think twice about kneeling in front of her, taking her hands in mine.

"No, I should know better. You are still healing."

She sighed and a small smile appeared on her lips as her grip on my hands tightened. Watching as she bit her bottom lip a little, it looked as if she was thinking of something, and I didn't want to pry. I just wanted to make sure she knew I was sorry and wouldn't try anything.

"Sam, if I asked you to do something for me, would you?"

She looked back up at me, her eyes a little red and glassy as if she had been crying.

"Anything. What is it?"

My stomach was doing summersaults as I thought about her question and how easy it was for me to answer. I would have done anything for this woman, whatever she asked and whatever the consequences, I would do it.

"Would you..."

She paused, biting her lip again and I wished in that moment I knew what was going through her head.

"Would you kiss me?"

My eyes widened, that wasn't at all what I was expecting. She had just run off leaving me on the dance floor after I had advanced a little, I thought it was because I had said the wrong thing. Perhaps it was the right thing? Was she still a little drunk? Was I? I wasn't sure anymore. Usually, fresh air would set me off into a stumbling mess, but I had no idea how Kim would be.

"Are you sure?" I asked, wanting to know if this was really what she wanted.

I would have kissed her instantly if it was any other day,

but seeing her after she had been crying, I didn't want her to think I was doing it out of pity. I wanted our potential first kiss to be perfect. Well, it wouldn't be our first kiss but our first kiss in a long, long time.

Without a word, she let go of my hands then placed them on my shoulders as she leaned inwards and brushed her lips gently across mine, inviting me.

My heart flipped and I was kissing her back in seconds. Wrapping my one arm around her waist and pulling her up so we could stand, I kept my lips locked on hers. She wrapped her arms around my neck as she pulled me down slightly and stood on her tiptoes. I had forgotten how small she was next to me as I used my free hand to place it on the back of her head, running my fingers in her hair.

Holy shit. I had forgotten how amazing she tasted as her tongue made its way into my mouth and I felt the heat rise on the back of my neck. A small moan escaped her lips as my hand around her waist lowered and palmed her ass.

I wanted at that moment to desperately take her back up to our hotel room and do as many things as I could to keep her making those little sounds. Bring her to the point of desire and lust. I wanted to feel her naked skin against mine as I put my lips between her legs. I would have done anything for her at that moment.

And as soon as I thought about it, she broke the kiss. Looking up at me through her eyelashes, I wanted to pull her in tightly again, carry her upstairs and have my way with her, but she stopped, and therefore I did, too.

"Shall we go upstairs?"

Again, my eyes widened as I was surprised this was even happening. Why was it happening? What had she come out here to think about? I didn't want to say no, but I had to know what was going on.

"I'm going to kick myself for this," I said under my breath as I still had my hands on her waist.

"I want to, and I would do anything to get you naked but, can I ask, why now?"

She didn't seem surprised by my question as if she knew I was going to ask it. Taking a step back, she fell back onto the bench, and I sat next to her. Although it was cold for an autumn night in Vancouver neither of us seemed to be bothered. That would change however shortly as the alcohol wore off.

"I won't lie and say I haven't thought about it. But I guess tonight has just made me feel a little braver than I usually would."

"Ah, so is this the drink talking or is this the Kimberly I know?"

"Ummm," laughing, she held her hands up in a surrender motion and smiled. "Probably a bit of both."

"Right, well in that case misses... we will be going upstairs, but to get you in some comfortable clothes and to put you to bed."

Her smile disappeared then as if she wasn't happy with my answer. I desperately wanted to do the right thing and be the right guy. I needed to treat her better as she deserved the world and not be the guy I was before.

"Kimberly, if maybe one day, when we do end up sleeping together," pausing, I moved a bit closer to her and placed a hand on her knee and whispered in her ear.

"I wanna fuck you senseless, but in order for me to do that, I need you to be sober and want you to want me as much as I want you."

Kissing her lightly on the side of her neck, she went still and moaned softly as I trailed the kisses up to her jawline then onto her lips.

"Is that alright with you?"

I almost growled, moving back, our noses touching. I watched her swallow hard as her blush reappeared on her cheeks as my hand moved up towards her thigh.

"That's, eh – that's fine by me."

She was breathless and I wanted to kiss her all over, bring her to the point of no return again and again. Friends didn't think of each other like this. I was starting to look at her as if she were the appetizer, main course, and dessert, especially in that dress.

"Let's go inside, it's getting a bit chilly."

Standing up, I linked my fingers into hers then led her back into the hotel and towards our room. The wedding sounded as if it was slowing down as guests made their way out of the room and towards the elevators. The happy couple was included in those leaving. When the groom saw us, he threw his arm over my shoulders as we waited to go upstairs.

"Not leaving already?" He asked, his breath smelling of whiskey.

"Ah, yeah, mate, gotta get to bed, you know, early session tomorrow."

He winked at me as he looked at Kimberly, his eyes drifting up and down her body. Although he was just married, he didn't seem to care very much as he ogled Kim. I wanted to punch him in that moment when he looked back up at me and tensed.

"Can we get a selfie?"

Rolling my eyes, I knew it was bound to happen, it always did. Fans would often ask for a picture with me. At this moment, as much as I wanted to say no and escape, I thought it would be best to agree. After all, we had gatecrashed his wedding.

Lining up beside him, he held the camera up, thankfully he cut Kim out of the frame, and snapped a few pictures, along with his other guests who recognized me.

Paula was going to have a field day tomorrow as there was no doubt these wouldn't go up on social media, people couldn't help themselves. We would have to come up with a cover story as to why I was even here.

"Night, boys."

"Yeah! Thanks, man!"

Once the elevator dinged, I was glad Kim pulled me towards the doors and out of their eyeline to head upstairs. She leaned into me a little as I wrapped a protective arm around her waist. She had been quiet since we got back inside. I was wondering if it was her maybe questioning what she had just asked to happen. Or if she regretted kissing me.

"Still friends?"

She lifted her head up and looked confused.

"Why wouldn't we be, idiot?"

"Well, after what just happened, I thought maybe you'd be a little mad."

She laughed a little as she went back to leaning her head against my shoulder.

"Sam, I think even when I was mad at you all these years, I would still have been your friend."

I let out a sigh at how grateful I was. It was a weight lifted off my shoulders. I never wanted to do anything to hurt or upset her. She deserved all the goodness in the world, and one way or another I was going to give it to her.

Fishing for the room key out of my pocket as we walked to the room, I kept my other arm snuggly around her. We headed inside and the first thing she did was kick off her heels then head into the bathroom. While she was busy, I searched through our bag for some comfy clothes then turned the AC over to heat. There was a slight chill in the room, and after being outside, we needed some heat.

"Shall I order room service?" I shouted.

"Will they still be serving?"

"It says 24 hours on the menu. I will see what I can get for us as I'm starving."

We had only eaten those burgers back at the café. If this were a regular day, I would have been on my fourth, maybe even fifth meal of the day. My stomach grumbled in protest as I flicked through the menu pages..

"Sam, can you unzip me please?"

She appeared beside me as I kept my eyes down on the menu, daring myself not to look. Turning around slowly, I looked at her as she moved her hair over one shoulder, and I felt my mouth run dry.

"No, getting ideas, misses," I joked, even though I was already full of ideas myself.

"Don't worry, Mr. Captain, I won't pounce on you."

Captain? Well, that would easily have sent me over the edge if I was a few inches deep inside her. After I unzipped her dress, only far enough for her to get undressed, she headed back into the bathroom with her pyjamas. Oddly enough, as much as I would have loved to see her in her underwear, I was looking forward to seeing her in her cozy mode.

Undoing the buttons of my shirt, I threw it on the back of a chair. After finally deciding what snacks we needed, I called down to the reception desk and ordered a bunch of options.

"Food's ordered."

"Oh, good, because I'm famished."

She stepped in the middle of the room with a make-up wipe in her hand and stared at me, her eyes traveling up and down as she took me in. Her eyes were almost ravenous. Before I even realized, I had crossed the bedroom and stood just a few inches away from her body.

The silk tank top left little to the imagination as I could make out the shapes of her breasts and her nipples pressing against the fabric. The shorts were shorter than I originally thought and if I could, I'd have ripped them off there and then.

The sexual tension in the room could have been cut with a knife as I watched her eyes lower to my lips. Unable to stop myself, I reached out, running my hands up and down her arms, while she placed a hand on my chest.

"Friends don't touch each other like this," she said under her breath, and I tried not to laugh.

"No, friends don't do this."

She took a step forward, closing the gap between us even more and I swore my heart skipped a beat. I wanted so badly to wrap my arms around her and pour myself into her. I didn't move as she went on her toes and started to kiss my neck, wrapping her other hand on the back of my neck, pulling me down towards her.

I couldn't ignore her pleas, I caved and kissed her passionately. Losing myself in her was exactly where I wanted to be. She moaned against my lips as I slipped one hand under her top and brushed my thumb against a nipple and pinched it lightly, rolling it between my thumb and finger. Kissing her deeply as she curved herself more into me, my other arm tightened around her waist as I leaned into her.

The heat and the lust was rising fast between us until a knock on the door stopped us suddenly.

"Room service."

I sighed against her lips as I reluctantly let go to answer

the door. Tipping the staff member, I pushed the rolling cart filled with trays of food and treats in, locking the door behind me. Kim sat on the edge of the bed, flushed and trying to catch her breath. If it wasn't for the fact food had arrived, I was pretty sure we would have ended up in bed together.

ow sitting on the edge of the bed, I tried to calm the heat that rose everywhere on my body. Sam was placing the plates of food on the small dining table in our room. I was too nervous to speak or even move. I wished he would put a shirt on to stop distracting me and making me think of things I wanted him to do to me.

He was even hotter than I remembered. His body was muscular in all the right places while his trousers sat perfectly on his hips. His right arm was covered in artwork. From what I could see it was mainly hockey themed and brightly colored.

"Well, move your ass and get some grub."

He pulled a chair out from the opposite side of the table and waited patiently for me to get up and join him. Once I was settled, he took the seat across from me and poured himself a glass of water then myself. He'd ordered a feast.

Chicken wings, a cheese board, crispy slices of bread, a large bowl of pasta with tomato sauce and a large bowl of chips. So many carbs, but Sam didn't seem bothered as he dipped his bread into some melted cheese.

"I think once I became an adult, I understood why cheese

is the superior food," he commented, with a mouthful of bread and I rolled my eyes laughing a little.

"I wouldn't know, not a big fan of cheese."

"What?! Kimmy, you're missing out."

He didn't seem at all fazed by our embrace earlier, the way he touched my skin or how we kissed each other. Friends most certainly didn't do any of that, but then again, were we really just friends? When I raced out of the wedding and sat outside to gather my thoughts, I kept returning to Luke's face. I felt like I was betraying him by having thoughts of another person.

But the words from my mother, her telling me that this pain would eventually fade, and I would be able to start living again, rang in my head. She was right, of course, she was right. Moms always knew best. And as I watched Sam enjoy his food, I couldn't help but smile at how simple it all was, how much I was enjoying this moment. But something was still bugging me.

"Sam, can I ask a question?"

"Always."

"Why um – why didn't you take me to prom?"

He stalled. His eyes dropped from mine and the air turned a little tense as he stopped eating. I wondered if I had completely ruined the moment, but I had to know. I had to understand why and until then, I knew I wouldn't allow myself to take the potential next step along this crazy unexpected path.

"I wanted to. I was all ready to go that night, tux on with that weird flower wrist thingy in the box and," he stopped, appearing to swallow a lump in his throat.

"You remember my dad?"

"Vaguely. He was the coach in school, right?"

"Yeah, well, we had this deal that if I wanted to go to prom,

I needed to pass some tests."

"But, you passed all your exams."

"They weren't those type of tests."

He kept his eyes lowered and didn't lift them up to look at me. He seemed a bit uneasy, and I wondered where this conversation was going. I just thought he didn't want to take me to prom because I wasn't the 'coolest' girl in school, being as I was a bit of an ice-skating geek.

"Well, I failed one of his tests and so, I was punished. That was, however, the last night he laid a hand on me."

My eyes widened at the sudden realization. Sam would often come to classes with a black eye, busted lip or some other injury and he would always say it was hockey practice or fighting with his mates. I never thought those injuries would be from his father. From what I remembered, the coach was always a pretty nice, chatty guy.

Reaching across the table, I took hold of his hand that rested on the edge and linked my fingers into his. His eyes rose to meet mine. They were a little glassy as if he was fighting back some tears. I didn't move or speak, I wanted him to know I was there and I was listening.

"I couldn't have you see me like that...and after that night, I went to live with my grandparents on my mom's side. I left, Kim, I ran away as fast as I could and as far as I could. I left Jane to fend for herself and I tried to go back, I did, but after graduation I headed off to college and never looked back."

When Jane died, I didn't see Samuel at the funeral, the entire town had showed up. I looked for him, as did Crystal and a few of the others. Jane was two years below us, but had become somewhat friends with Joseph. Everyone in town knew her. She was the quiet shop clerk at the market who was hoping to become a vet one day.

"I'm sorry you felt like you could never tell me."

"Why would I? You didn't need that kinda baggage and I was such a dick to you in the end. I ignored you, blocked your number and just left you, in the dark, alone. Like I did Jane."

I didn't think twice before I pushed off my seat and went to give him the tightest hug I could muster. Not a second passed and he pulled me onto his lap as he wrapped his arms around me.

"What happened to your sister wasn't your fault."

Burying his head into my shoulder, I felt his heart race against my chest. I realized in that moment, he wasn't the same guy I met back in school. He was broken and needed healing just as much as I did.

"None of what happened is your fault."

Leaning back, I cupped his face and watched as he studied me. Wondering what was going on in his head, I gently stroked his face then kissed him lightly on the lips.

This wasn't a kiss of wanting or where I was hoping something would lead off from it, I just wanted to give him some comfort.

After letting go, I wrapped my arms around his shoulders and hugged him tightly as he hugged me back. We stayed in this position for as long as he needed it, and it was only when he started loosening his grip did I let go.

"I know you may not believe me, but I am truly, deeply sorry for the pain and hurt I caused you."

"It was a long time ago, Sam."

"I know, but I still need you to hear me say I'm sorry and know that I mean it. Leaving you behind was one of the hardest things I ever had to do." He placed a hand on my cheek and rubbed his thumb across my skin as I stared at him a little baffled. I could hear as well as see the sincerity of his words in the way his eyes glistened.

"As soon as my manager told me to go home I had a

feeling I'd bump into you. I didn't think it would be on my first day back though, but I am so grateful that you spoke to me."

"Well, I wasn't going to just ignore you – Although, I did think about it."

"Ahh, but my good looks kept calling you back."

He winked at me with a cheerful teasing smile, and I just wanted to melt into his arms there and then. Despite how much he had gone through, he always seemed to have a smile on his face or at least appeared to be positive. I knew deep down it was because his lifestyle gave him stress, but his smiles were contagious.

"Shall we finish the food and head to bed?"

Reluctantly, I slipped off his lap and went to grab my phone to see the time. And it was extremely late or was it really early in the morning, either way, the fatigue I had been fighting all day was coming in waves.

"Sounds good to me."

Once we finished the food and Sam had changed into a pair of sweatpants, we climbed into the rather large Queen-sized bed. Oddly enough I was glad it had a lot of space in it. This would be the first time since Luke that I slept next to a man that wasn't my husband, but Sam kept his distance.

"I hope you don't snore," I said, rolling on my side towards him.

He laughed a little as he turned on a small lamp beside the bed, giving the room a warm orange glow.

"I hope you don't either." He winked at me and got himself comfortable.

"Well, goodnight then."

"Goodnight, Kim."

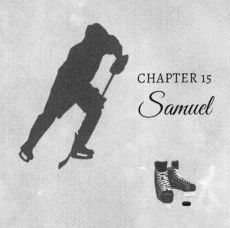

CHAPTER 15
Samuel

The constant vibrating of a phone against the bedside table woke me from my sleep and I flipped the phone over to put it on silent. I didn't want it disturbing Kim anymore as she shifted a little in the space next to me. At some point we had become closer, I found her back tucked up next to me. I would have cuddled in more if the knocking on the hotel room door didn't start.

Knocking gently at first then increasingly getting louder and louder the longer I took to move. Kim started to move as she lifted her head up and turned a little to look at me sleepily.

"Is that the door?"

Now there was another vibrating noise in the room, this time it was Kim's phone was lighting up with an unknown mobile number.

"SAMUEL JONES, OPEN THIS DOOR RIGHT NOW!"

I thought for a split second my mother had tracked me down, but nope, it was in fact the women who had pretty much become my mother. Paula. Paula was shouting behind the closed door.

"Oh, fuck."

Panic rolled over me as I let go of Kim and lifted my phone up, to too many missed calls to count, voicemails and many many texts from Paula as well as my entire PR team. I knew what this was. And this was bad.

Kim pushed herself up and rested her back against the headboard as she took hold of her phone. The knocking still continued. I was a little scared to open it, I knew Paula was going to ring my neck. I really didn't want her first meeting with Kim to be of Paula kicking my ass.

"Eh, Sam, you may want to answer that."

Yes, I better answer as the knocking was now turning into hammering and more shouting came from Paula. I was pretty sure security would have been called by now judging by how loud she was. Getting up, I nervously went to the door, unlocking it and as I opened it Paula, Katelyn and Matthew came bursting in. My entire PR team was here.

"Well, you really fucked this one up, haven't you!" Paula shouted as she stepped into the room. I swear the vein on her forehead was bigger than ever before. It was very likely it might just explode this time.

"You made a complete utter mess in one single fucking night! Sam, do you know how hard it is to hide a player like you away from the media?! IT'S EXTREMELY DIFFICULT!!!"

"Sorry, Paula, I, eh..."

She tossed her hand up at me to make me stay quiet. Paula usually did the shouting and screaming. Katelyn was more or less the one who dealt with the press releases. But then Matthew... I wasn't always sure what he really did, other than listen and take notes.

"Now the media is having a field day! Captain of the Vancouver Devils hiding in a small city with champion figure skater Kimberly Morgan," she paused to look at Kim who was dumbfounded, still in bed. "Lovely to meet you by the way, I've heard a lot about you."

The Paula switch, it was scary how quickly she changed her moods. With Kim, she was as calm and collected as she could be, but then she turned her face back to me, her anger almost to a boiling point.

"It was just a harmless selfie, we can easily spin it and say I was here visiting friends and they just happened to be guests or something for the wedding and I was the plus one."

"Katelyn, show him."

Katelyn handed over the iPad she always carried and swiped across to show not the selfies at the wedding, but photographs of Kimberly and I outside the hotel, in a very compromising situation. Looking at Kim now who seemed to be scrolling through her phone wearing the same expression as me, I knew we had just seen the same thing.

"Oh, no," was all she said as she continued to look through her phone.

Both of us realized at the same time what a mess this was now going to create. Sitting down on the edge of the bed, I flicked through the photographs. There were multiple ones of us sitting on the bench talking, some of us kissing, my hand on her ass then on her thigh. I had been stupid to think there wasn't going to be some photographic evidence of me at some point.

"Word is, someone spotted you at some café and followed you to the hotel. They were lying in wait. The photographs are everywhere. Chris isn't impressed either, Sam."

Paula finally appeared to calm down. Chris was my manager and the one in charge of the hockey team, he was most likely going to kill me as this had now turned into a big media mess. I had to somehow fix it. For the team and for Kim.

"What do we do now then?"

Kim asked as she got up out of bed and wrapped herself in one of the hotel bathrobes. She didn't look at me for a minute and in that minute, I felt a little shameful. This was my fault, and I should have known better.

"We have a few ideas, but one of them, we think is the best choice to make," Katelyn said as she took the iPad back.

"We should spin this angle; you guys have a history together and if we use that to our advantage. Get you back in the rink and have Kim show up to some of your games, watch your comeback and we tell the story that you are both dating."

"But we're not. We're just friends."

Kimberly stepped in and I felt like I had been stabbed in my heart. We may not have been dating, but I was hoping at some point we could get to that stage in our relationship.

"Yes, we understand that Miss Morgan, but we now need to back track and fix this. If you had both been discreet and not sat outside, then this might have been avoided. But now we are in damage control."

Paula was always assertive and knew just what to do with these types of situations as it hadn't been her first, especially not with me. I felt bad when I thought about how many times we had to spin a line because I had been caught red-handed with a woman, worse when it wasn't the person I was meant to be dating.

"So, how long have we got to put up this charade?"

"Ummm, give or take a few weeks and then we can slowly let the 'relationship' fade. Sounds good to you?"

I didn't make eye contact with Kim as I was starting to feel maybe last night was just because of the drinking and she was already regretting it. Katelyn and Matthew started work almost instantly, calling for room service to come and clean up the dirty plates, bring up breakfast and coffee. They set their laptops up on the table, working on the mess I had made once again.

We sat in silence for the most part. Kimberly changed in the bathroom shortly after I did. It was a little awkward now as she tapped her fingers loudly on her phone and ignored all the phone calls that came through. We figured out the unknown number that had been calling was Paula. How she got Kim's number I'd never know as that woman was good at finding out things and keeping secrets. She should have worked for the FBI rather than the NHL.

"Right, we've booked you an interview with channel six sports news. We will have you talk about your break, how you met each other and what's next on the cards for your hockey career."

"I'm sorry, but we? We won't be doing that. I must head back; I have a skating lesson to teach."

Kim stood with her arms crossed as she stared Paula down. I didn't blame her though; she had been tossed into this world because of my stupidity. Paula didn't stand down and for a minute I thought it was going to become a potential show down until Paula sat down.

"Alright, Matthew, can you organize a car for Miss Morgan? Sam, you are to stay here and prepare for an interview. With Miss Morgan's permission, is it alright if we go ahead as planned?"

"Honestly, I'd rather not be mentioned. I will have to deal with all the backlash when I get back home. So, if we can keep my name down to a minimum the better."

She was pissed and I knew once this day ended, I'd try and talk to her about all of this, what was a good idea and what wasn't. I hated how my celebrity status would ruin my relationships, friendships or otherwise. Granted, most of that had been my fault, but I wanted to have Kim in my life, I didn't want to lose her again.

"I will try my best to steer the interview away from you Kim." I stood and tried to move towards her, but she in turn stepped backwards.

"How long until the car?" She asked, almost looking through me.

"A few minutes. It will pick you up from the staff entrance, to avoid the media that is out by the entrance." Katelyn spoke before she went back to her phone call.

Grabbing her things, Kim headed out the door without even uttering a goodbye. I went to rush after her, and Paula grabbed my wrist shaking her head.

"Leave her be. I warned you, Sam."

"I can't just let her run off without at least talking to her."

"You must, for now. You can call her later, but for now, we need to get you prepped and ready."

Sighing and admitting defeat, I did as I was told and began preparing for the interview that would now make or break my career as there would be questions as to why I'm not in this season.

CHAPTER 16
Kimberly

The drive back was a quiet one. I assumed the uber driver was sworn to secrecy, as he barely said a word other than hello. During the ride I tried desperately not to flick through my phone. Crystal had already called me ten times by the time we reached the BC-99, and was heading home to Merrifort.

I had managed to get the rink manager on the phone after a couple of tries and asked if I could take a few days leave. She had seen the news and although it sounded like she wanted to ask a million questions, no doubt to tell the local book club filled with gossip, she agreed to my emergency leave.

I hated canceling lessons, the girls needed me, but I needed time to process yesterday. I would either offer extra hours or refund the girls' parents to make up for it. To my surprise, once I sent the group chat a message about not being in until Friday, they all seemed to understand. The girls were a little grateful for the extra time to work on their routines.

When the uber driver pulled up next to my drive, I wasn't surprised to see Crystal sitting on the porch. The moment I stepped out of the car, Daisy came to greet me.

"Fun time?" Crystal asked with a smile on her face as I walked up the porch steps.

I didn't say a word, just headed on inside. I was exhausted, I needed a shower and a cup of coffee. I had raced out of that hotel room so fast; I didn't even have a chance to brush my teeth. I didn't think my morning would have begun in a PR mess up.

"You okay, hun?"

Crystal followed me in as I plonked myself down on my sofa. Daisy joined me instantly and placed her head on my lap. I felt this overwhelming need to cry, shout, or maybe both, I wasn't sure. Pouring a cup of coffee for me, Crystal held it out to me shortly after and sat next to me and Daisy. I wasn't sure where to start.

Explaining how the day went and the fact I did enjoy myself, there was no denying it. Deep down the teenager who was madly in love with Samuel was over the moon to be in his company again.

"So, you left without speaking to him?"

"Yep. I didn't know what to say, I was so mad and upset. I didn't think for one second this was going to happen, all I wanted to do was go back to work and live out my days."

"Wow. You sound a bit like an old lady there, maybe you should move to the woods in a cottage and adopt loads of cats." Crystal joked, trying to raise a laugh out of me.

"Mind you, that does sound peaceful."

She finished off and that did make me laugh a little. Megan, Lacy, Jasmine, and she would make the perfect little witches hiding in the woods. Like those magical witch sisters in Charmed or Practical Magic.

"I'm sorry your morning ended this way, but honestly Kim, you can't blame him for this. Yes, maybe you shouldn't be making out in open public spaces, but hey if it's what the heart wants."

"It's not what the heart wants."

"Oh, piss off will you. You cannot deny there is some serious chemistry between you two and I know, I know Luke was your great love, but Sam is your first love and that means something. I remember how hung up you were over him."

"You will remember then how badly heartbroken I was after the whole prom thing, which by the way I now know it wasn't his fault."

"Oh?"

"Sorry, I can't say as it's his business, but it was for a good reason."

"Then what's stopping you from taking a step with him? Is it Luke?"

Was it Luke? What was the reason I didn't want to move forward? Why was I stuck in this rut I had put myself in? I knew the drink helped give me some liquid courage, but those feelings must have been there, buried deep within me. Luke would often jokingly say I was still madly in love with Sam when he caught me watching his games or reading the news.

I wasn't, at least I wasn't back then. Luke was all I saw; from the moment we met till this very moment. And yet, Sam had sparked something inside me. Maybe that's why I had gotten so mad over the pretend dating thing. Maybe I didn't want to pretend and now I wasn't sure where to go.

"Look babes, I need to get to the café before Lacy shoots me for leaving her there to tend to customers. But give me a call later okay? Get some rest, have a shower, and just chill. Maybe text Sam later and see what's what."

Of course, Crystal was the levelheaded one and the one who always brought me back down to earth. After some sleep and a wash, I was sure to feel better.

After settling into bed for a couple of hours, I couldn't get those images of Sam and I together out of my mind. I had popped my phone on silent and double locked my front and back door. My mother would try to come over unannounced. I wanted to avoid everyone for as long as possible.

Scrolling through my phone, I wondered how Sam was getting on. Despite how much I wanted to ignore it, I turned on my bedroom television and went to channel six. There he was, looking as handsome as ever, if not a bit more than usual.

"So, Mr. Jones, tell us, who the mystery woman is? We've got some guesses, but can you confirm to us if it is the famous figure skater, Kimberly Morgan?"

Sam chuckled a little and I took that as a sign he was thinking of how to respond. He'd done the same thing while we were at the café, and I asked him some awkward question.

"I think it would do a disservice to that lady if I were to expose her, don't you think?"

"But you're currently one of the most eligible bachelors and we need to know if you're off the market."

"Ha ha! Well, Olivia, I can assure you I am not still on the market. This relationship is still new, and I'd rather not spoil it by talking about it all over the media."

The interviewer smiled at him and could see by his face and tone, he was not going to give anything away. I was grateful, he wasn't publicly announcing me and he was trying to shut the speculation down. He had stuck to his guns and wasn't going to tell everyone what was going on. Even if they had guessed right that it was me in those photographs.

I contemplated calling him as this was a repeat of his interview. Would it be possible for us to move past all this? I still wanted him to come to Joe's wedding and was looking forward to maybe dancing with him again. But, it wouldn't have been a problem if he said no and moved away again. It would make sense, he has his career after all.

"What's next with hockey for you? You've been off for a few weeks now haven't you?"

I didn't intend to listen to the interview after the conversation changed, but I had always been interested in hockey. I'd sometimes sneak into his games when they were local. I always had a feeling Luke knew but never said anything. I was just happy most of the time to see Sam had succeeded in what he always wanted to do.

"We shall see what happens. The NHL has many plans for me. I am currently in the process of organizing a little charity hockey match in my hometown. It's to raise some money for their local kids hockey teams and ice skaters."

"That sounds amazing! Will you be inviting us at channel six to cover it?"

"Of course, Olivia, you are, after all, my favorite newscaster."

It was news to me that he was looking to organize a charity event, but then again I hadn't heard from him most of the day. I was partly to blame for not sending him a text or anything, but he hadn't sent one either.

IT HAD BEEN over three weeks since Sam and I had really spoken or seen each other. We had a few texts back and forth, but didn't talk about anything serious. I wasn't even sure if he was coming back to town for a while. Our conversations weren't even conversations, time zones made it difficult to keep track of replies and we only ever got as far as how are you.

Sitting down at my office desk at the rink, I rubbed my temples feeling a headache coming on. Rachel, the rink manager, had asked me multiple questions about this charity event and if I had any idea about it, when it was going to happen and anything else she could think to ask me.

I had no idea.

Sam hadn't really replied to any of my questions, including the ones about if we were still 'dating' as far as the media knew. I was thankful Joseph and Beth's wedding was in a week's time as it gave me something else to think about.

My dress Sam had demanded I have from that dress shop arrived a few days ago and was hanging up in my closet. I was still unsure if I should wear it. Joe said he liked it, and Beth didn't seem to mind either, if anything she seemed happy. I had sorted myself out and wasn't being a mess or overbearing, unlike her bridesmaids.

"Kim."

Rachel popped her head round my office door, and I sighed, dreading what else she was going to try and talk to me about. I was a little fed up with the Sam this, Sam that conversations.

"Did you say your girls will be here for a lesson today?"

Rachel was a pretty decent manager, she had taken over the rink when her dad passed away. Luckily, we had grown up together via the rink. She never competed, but I always thought she should have, she was a natural on the ice. She would always say, she was better at bossing people around then the other way round.

"Yeah, they're due in an hour."

"Eh, right, ummm," she lowered her eyes, and I wasn't entirely sure what the problem was. "There are some news crews here and umm some of Mr. Jones' team, they need the rink."

"So, I must cancel my girls for the sake of the media? Are you joking?"

"Well, if you can ask them to come a little later it will be fine."

"No, Rachel. I will not be doing that."

Shoving my chair away from my desk, I barged past Rachel and headed down towards the rink. There was no way my girls were missing out simply because some camera crew needed to take photographs or whatever they were doing. They could wait.

As I reached the steps down the stairs, I could hear multiple voices and I stopped for a moment. I'd be really making a mess if I just showed up downstairs kicking off when I was already being mentioned in the papers.

Reaching the bottom step, I paused, unsure if I should push the doors open that led into the arena. I'd make a fool out of myself if I did start arguing with them. No, my girls didn't deserve to be pushed aside, they had competitions coming up.

Standing up straight and taking a calming breath, I pushed the doors opened and stepped in. The lights were already blinding as there were several more dotted around the rink to make it appear almost daylight.

I recognized Katelyn and Matthew as they stood outside the rink along with Olivia from channel six. Looking around, I tried not to see if I could spot Sam. It wasn't too surprising when I noticed he wasn't anywhere near. A soft sigh escaped as I allowed a tiny bit of disappointment to creep in at not seeing him.

"I hope you're not going to step on the ice without the correct footwear," I said, clearing the small space between us.

"Oh, Miss Morgan, lovely to see you again." Katelyn smiled at me a little too brightly as Matthew just nodded hello. "I hope you don't mind the intrusion. We've invited Olivia here to do a feature on the rink to prepare for the charity match."

"Nice to meet you."

"It's wonderful to meet you, Kimberly. I used to watch your shows with my mom, such a shame you stopped skating."

Olivia seemed nice enough, for a television personality. I had met many interviewers in the years I competed and often or not, I found them arrogant and pushy. She stood tall in a beautifully tailored gray suit and skyscraper black heels.

"Again, I must advise you guys don't go onto the ice. It's just been cleaned and can be a little dangerous for those who aren't used to it."

"Yeah, Mr. Jones did say we needed to be careful," Matthew jumped in as he looked nervously at the rink. "We are just here to get some footage. We won't keep you guys too long, Rachel mentioned you have a class shortly."

"Yes, I have my girls coming. They are training for the regionals next month and we can't really afford to miss any lessons."

"Say, I have an idea." Oliva spoke up as if a light bulb went off in her head. "Could we maybe get some shots of you training the girls?"

"You would need their parents' permission to film them, Olivia." Katelyn took the words right out of my mouth.

"Oh, I'm sure they will say yes! What parent doesn't enjoy seeing their kids on the television? That is, if it's alright with you?"

Standing there unsure of how this conversation had been flipped to asking me to be on film, to be part of the feature, I felt my palms grow sweaty. The last time I had been in front of any camera was during my last championship, I came in third,

Bronze. My coach made out it was due to Luke's health and my head not being in the game anymore. The truth was, I just didn't want to do it anymore.

"If the parents agree, then I am ok with it, but you cannot ask the girls any questions."

"Deal, thanks, Kim! This will be so great, and it means we can truly show a wider picture about the teams that need sponsorships and stuff."

Granted, the girls would go far if they had the backing of a company or someone who was willing to sponsor their career. I had valued my sponsors at the time, they helped when I needed new costumes, skates, or travel expenses to comps.

"Katelyn."

Once Matthew and Olivia had moved out of earshot, to continue talking about the filming, I assumed, I wanted to get Katelyn's attention.

"Is he here?"

"Mr. Jones? No, sorry, he's at HQ prepping for another press conference. He's got a game this Saturday and needs to train."

"Where's the game?"

"Videotron Centre arena. It's his comeback game so they wanted to make sure it was a big one."

Lowering my eyes, I felt slightly disappointed. It would have been nice to see him here and maybe we could clear the air, discuss what happened back at the hotel and maybe move past it. Katelyn went back on her phone and began calling some number and as I began to leave, she took hold of my hand.

"Yes, I need the plane ready for Friday. Yes, Miss Morgan will be attending the game."

My eyes widened as I hadn't suggested anything like that or even been asked if I wanted to go. Clearly Katelyn liked to take charge, the same as Paula it seemed. She hung up the phone a minute later and smiled at me as if she had done me a favor.

"Eh, Katelyn, I can't just up and leave. My brother's wedding is next weekend and I'm needed here."

"Yes, and I believe Mr. Jones will be attending the wedding. We already have it booked in the planner; he will make the return flight with you."

I wasn't used to being told what to do, or what was happening. I was pretty good at planning my own things or at least doing things my way. She smiled at me a little wider, happy with her choice, before letting go of my hand and left me standing there questioning if this was a good idea.

"Wait. Does he even know?" I shouted.

"No, it's a surprise," she shouted back and Olivia's eyes picked up as she asked Katelyn what we had talked about.

CHAPTER 17
Samuel

I lost count how many news anchors and interviews I had done by the time we reached the hotel in Vancouver. My feet ached, my head pounded and there was a stabbing pain behind my eyes. All I wanted to do was sleep and yet, Chris and Paula continued discussing my big game tomorrow night.

Chris asked a million questions about Kimberly and why she hadn't been to any of the interviews. What was she to me and did she even matter? I lost count of the number of times I was ready to lose my shit and smash his teeth in. If it wasn't for Paula I would have.

I hadn't seen the boys yet, not since Chris benched me. Sighing again, I knew deep down there was going to be some issues with my return. After all, I was still captain, and my sub-captain would need to back the hell down when I skated onto the ice tomorrow.

"I've organized breakfast for tomorrow morning with the boys. Sam, you need to make amends."

Chris ordered while he stuffed his face with a burger. I was too tired to eat and didn't really care what he wanted or what his feelings were.

"Sam, it would be a good idea to apologize to Jason. You know, you did punch him in the face then almost beat him senseless." Paula placed a hand on my shoulder and looked at me with worrisome eyes.

"Alright, I will apologize. Can we leave it now? I need sleep."

"Sure, buddy, Paula and I need to go over a few more things, just be down here at nine tomorrow." Again, Chris commanded, I could almost make out his full sentence behind his fries. The man would choke talking and eating at the same time as he did.

Finishing my drink and cramming the last bit of food in my mouth, I left them to talk. Heading upstairs and down the corridor to my hotel room, my feet dragged. I was beyond exhausted. Feeling grateful when the large king size bed greeted me, I couldn't wait to jump in the shower, wash off the airplane smell and climb in.

Turning on the television for some background noise, I flicked to the NHL sports channel. It wasn't surprising to see my face as lights and cameras flash when I entered this hotel. I wouldn't have been surprised either if they were still stationed outside waiting, like vultures, for when the rest of the team arrived.

We were at the top of our game, champions for the last three seasons. Since Jason took my place, we were losing our scoring rep and winning streak. Maybe that's why they wanted me back so soon as I had thought I'd be off for at least another six months.

Once showered, I sighed as I climbed into the comfortable bed and almost knocked myself out as I yanked the bed sheets upwards. Why hotels insisted on tucking the sheets in at the bottom so tightly I'd never know. I was grateful when my eyes started to get heavy and I switched the bedside lamp off. My mind wondered, thinking back to the hotel room I stayed in with Kimberly and how I was missing her company.

"CAN we just all let bygones be bygones, Sam has realized the error of his dickheaded ways and now we have to kick ass at our game tonight!"

Louis was my left-wing man and the only one I could rely on throughout the entire team. He reminded me of a hyperactive puppy most of the time, always bouncing his leg, playing with something, or talking rather fast. Slapping me on the back as I tried to drink my coffee, he almost caused me to choke on it. Jason rolled his eyes from across the table while the other four, Duncan, James, Ryan, and Noah kept their heads down and continued eating their breakfast.

"Look man, I know I'm an ass and I shouldn't have thrown a punch and stuff at you. I do apologize."

"You could have at least hit properly, you hit like a girl." Jason teased as he nudged Ryan, which in turn made him awkwardly laugh.

Rolling my eyes at the attempt of a joke, I was a little glad the air was clearing as we continued our breakfast. Chris sat silently for once, at the head of the table as he flicked through today's newspaper. Our team's group photo was in the middle spread with many predictions and guesses over the upcoming game's score dotted around it.

"So, Sam, what's this girl of yours like?" Louis asked.

"Eh, she's alright, yeah."

"Where'd you find her?"

James asked next as all eyes fell to me. James was just as loud as Louis, almost. He and Duncan were brothers and they had pretty much followed each other throughout life. He was known as our white knight, the first one to always try and do something noble. It's why so many women throw themselves at him, but alas he was married.

Duncan however, was the complete opposite. Quiet, the dark horse of the group. He would watch, listen, and take notes of what was going on. Duncan was the first one to say when I needed to sort my stuff out and I respected him more for doing that.

"She, um, we used to date back in high school and bumped into each other back home."

I wasn't going to lie to the boys, as I needed to make this a new chapter of my life. Fix the mistakes I had made, start to treat them as my teammates, and not just boys I played a game with. That's the attitude I had before, and it ended up with me being 'removed'. We were meant to be like family, Paula had made sure to drill that in my head a lot recently and I was starting to believe her.

"She will be at the rink when we do the charity match. She teaches figure skating there."

The conversation died down shortly after which made me happy. I glanced down to my phone, hoping Kim had answered my last few texts, but alas, there was silence. I had really pissed her off back at the hotel, but I didn't think she'd still be mad three weeks later.

If I sent her another text, it may become slightly creepy and annoying, neither of which I wanted to be. But then I didn't want to come across as uninterested and not make any effort.

"When the Montreal Canadians get in then, Chris?" Jason asked as he finished his food.

"They should be arriving any minute. They are staying in a different hotel though boys, so none of you can cause anymore PR grief. We have enough of that already."

Chris directed his eyes at me, and I just smiled innocently. As our manager, he was allowed to be angry and annoyed at us, but he'd been with us for nearly five years now, so he knew how we were and was used to it.

"Take out all the fun, Chris," Louis joked.

> Hey, I'm just checking in. Sorry, probably being really annoying now.

> I've got my comeback game tonight.

> I will make a goal for you.

A text message, as per my better judgment. But as I sat there listening to the boys having conversations about their lives, James was talking about his wife Emily to Ryan, it made me feel slightly lonely. I missed hearing Kimberly's voice.

The tiny chat bubble showed up and I felt my heart skip. Excitement brewed, we hadn't replied to each other at the same time in weeks. I sat there anxiously looking at my phone screen, only no reply. The bubble disappeared and my smile dropped.

"Careful now, Sam, looks like someone murdered your puppy."

Louis again, always trying to make light of a situation. Shaking my head, I ignored him and locked my phone. Maybe Kim will reply to me later, or tomorrow... Or never.

Once breakfast was over, Chris ordered us all to hit the hotel gym for an hour then get ready for the game. Even if it was at least nine hours away, he always wanted us to be prepped and ready to go.

A workout session was always a good idea. However, clearing your head, sometimes would turn into a challenge itself as we all competed to see who could bench the most weights or run the most laps.

CHAPTER 18
Kimberly

Showing my passport at the gate, my hands shook a little as the nerves started to kick in. I had never flown first class, even during my competition days, the most I would get were business class. Katelyn had met me at the gate the following day after we spent a good three hours filming shots as the girls trained.

I did think at first the parents would have been angry. But since my sudden shot back to fame, they were more than happy to have the girls included in the feature, if anything it made the girls work harder and show their skills more.

Olivia had refrained from asking me any questions other than how long we had been training, what the charity match would mean to the girls and the rink, and how people can help get involved.

Our small town needed the publicity. We had so many amazing talented ice skaters and hockey players, as well as other talented youths, they needed to be seen.

"Right this way, ma'am."

The flight attendant guided me to my rather large seat, way too large for just little old me and took hold of my overnight bag, putting it up in the overhead compartment. Katelyn sat on the opposite row to me and promptly got out her laptop and began working on whatever she needed to do.

She had suddenly become in charge of me and I wasn't too sure if I was okay with it. Sending a quick selfie of myself to my girls group chat, Crystal was the first to respond, closely followed by Lacy and Megan as close seconds. They sent many emojis of excitement then a selfie with Crystal, Lacy and my sweet Daisy came through.

I felt awful for leaving her alone again. She had become so used to me being home, I hated being away from her. She was my comfort. But I knew she wouldn't mind as Crystal would spoil her rotten.

> Safe travels baby girl! Let us know when you land and see that sweet hockey ass. ;)

Rolling my eyes at Megan's text to the group, I locked my phone and got myself comfortable. It was a five-hour flight to Quebec City. I had brought a book along for the flight, knowing full well I'd be able to finish it in the five hours. I hoped I didn't fall asleep so I could read. Which is what I ended up doing an hour into our journey.

The flight attended woke me up as we began our descent, and this was the only time flying made me nervous. The landing seemed alright, but I was glad when my feet touched normal ground. We headed out the terminal towards the car Katelyn had arranged for us.

"We will be heading to the hotel where Sam and his team are staying. He won't be there now though, he will be off training. You should be able to see him during half time or after the game."

Katelyn was a very assertive woman, very proud of her job. She definitely was the envy of most girls in her school just by her looks. Tall, with beautiful long blond hair, bright blue eyes, and a sweet smile to boot. She looked like one of those girls you either dreamt of being or the one you tried to avoid in hopes she didn't bully you.

I hated judging a person by the way they looked, especially as I was now slowly getting to know her. She was sweet, happy to answer my questions and reassure me at any moment. I thought we would perhaps become friends, should Sam and I stay in each other's lives, maybe.

Arriving at the hotel and using the underground carpark entrance to avoid the crowds of media presence. Most of them had stationed themselves outside, most likely hoping to get that shot they needed. We headed up to my room, Katelyn deciding she should come with me just to help me get settled in, even if I was only going to be here for two nights.

"You have my number if you need anything. I've had one of the girls bring up some clothes for you for tonight."

"I, eh, I already have clothes."

"Yeah, I know, but you need to be seen wearing Sam's number, to show support and stuff. You can pair it with a pair of jeans. Oh, and stick a long-sleeved top underneath, you and I both know the rinks are freezing," she answered, smiling as she headed towards the door. Before reaching the door, she spun on her heel and turned to look at me, pausing as if to stop herself from saying what she wanted. "I will see you at seven. Get some sleep, order room service, shower, do whatever you want, but please stay in this room. We can't have the media catching wind you're here."

"I didn't know I was a secret."

"Not a secret, just eh, a surprise."

Winking and smiling at me, she left me alone, standing in the middle of the rather large, family sized hotel room. Way too big for just me, I would have been happy with just a nice bed and a television. Deciding a bath would be the nicest option, I ordered room service first as I was starving as well as a bottle of red wine, to calm my nerves.

Why was I even worried? It wasn't as if I hadn't seen Sam before. We had our hands all over each other last time.

Shortly after eating the most beautiful chicken dinner I have had in a long time, I ran a bubble bath and poured myself a glass.

If I was going to be here for a few hours, I might as well indulge myself. Hearing my phone buzz, I assumed it was the group chat as I had sent many selfies of my room, my food, the bathtub, and that instagrammable photograph of holding my glass of wine with the bubbles, but it was Sam.

My fingers hovered over the keypad, wondering how I was meant to respond. If Katelyn had said I was a surprise, would it have been a good idea to reply? She said he would be busy. Looking at the time, it had just gone midday. It wouldn't do harm if I did reply though, I could just make out I was out walking Daisy or on my way to work.

As I began to type my message, I stopped. I wasn't sure if Katelyn or Paula would be annoyed with me if I did reply. No, I will leave it, keep the suspense there.

ARRIVING at the arena made my nerves really amp themselves up. My one leg bounced up and down on the spot as I took my seat in the row with Katelyn and Matthew. Paula was nowhere to be seen, but the seat next to me was left open for her. The row in front of us housed the other teammates' girlfriends or wives, I wasn't sure. It seemed everyone had a person.

There was so much nervous energy going through me, causing me to adjust the number three black with red and yellow stripes hockey jersey. It had bunched itself up on my back and made me feel incredibly uncomfortable. I felt grateful that Katelyn reminded me to wear another layer underneath as this rink was in fact ice cold, worse than the rink back home.

As the lights went down low and music began blaring out through the speakers, the first team was announced. The Montreal Canadiens, four-time world champions and the opponent for today's match. This wasn't a competitive match, a purely friendly one to announce Sam's return.

They came out almost guns blazing in their blue and red jerseys and the crowd went wild. Ice hockey was such an amazing sport and huge in Canada, it even beat out the NFL sometimes by the amount of people that watched the games. The team waved and blew kisses at the crowd clearly enjoying the sudden popularity. Then the music changed again and out came The Vancouver Devils and first on the ice was Samuel.

He had his jersey with a large C on the front, stating he was captain again. His alternate, Jason, followed closely behind. I thought the crowd had been pleased to see the other team, but nothing prepared me for the screaming and shouting. I swore some fans were crying as they saw Sam and his team join the others on the ice.

Trying to keep my head low, I didn't really want him spotting me just yet, I could feel my nerves growing again. I was just there to watch, I didn't want to throw him off his game. Luckily, he didn't spot me as he just went to huddle with his team and manager before the bell sounded off.

"I'm going to take that one home tonight, girls, I'm telling you, tonight is the night. I'm getting him back."

"Aha, Stace, good luck with that, you know Sam will just say no again."

My ears perked up as I listened in closely to the girls in front of me having a conversation, clearly unbothered that everyone could hear them.

"Nope, not tonight, he's having me all to himself."

"Best of luck, hun, I heard his new girlfriend is here."

"Ha! I will take her out of the game easily, I know what he likes and she most certainly can't keep his attention."

My blood began to boil a little as I heard them begin talking about me. Katelyn had lowered her phone and was listening as well. Both of us gave each other the side eye as she shook her head, mouthing 'no'. Clearly she knew I wanted to say something. Even if I wasn't really Sam's girlfriend, I still couldn't continue hearing them talk about my friend. Especially not as if he was a piece of meat. If this was the other way round and a guy was talking about a girl this way, there would be hell to pay.

Leaning forward, they both turned as they sensed me there and the one girl's eyes widened as she noticed me sitting there, where the one named 'Stace' seemed oblivious.

"I think you will find; we don't sleep when I am entertaining him."

A wide smile crept up as I looked at them both, Stace finally realizing who I was, and a flash of red went down her neck. Her friend lowered her eyes instantly and went to turn away, but Stace didn't seem to want to back down.

"You are just his flavor of the week, he will tire of you and come running back to me."

"I'm sorry, who are you? Are you some groupie or something?" I taunted, having none of it. "Because I know he's never called your name out when we fuck."

Katelyn and Matthew bit back a laugh from beside me and

the other girls started to turn around slowly, each listening closely. Stace started to stand up from her seat, trying to look intimidating and something inside me was ready to snap.

"Who the hell do you think you are?!" She shouted at me, and I laughed a little.

"Could you sit down please, I'm trying to watch my *boyfriend* play."

The tension could be cut like a knife, and I wanted desperately to knock her down a few pegs. She was clearly not used to not getting her way. But even if Sam and I were only fake dating, the idea of some random girl having him in her bed made me uncontrollably angry.

Her friend started to pull her down by the wrist and she fought her friend, the redness in her neck now traveling up to her face. I would have quite easily continued if it wasn't for the goal buzzer going off. The entire crowd roared together as Sam's team scored another goal.

So far, the match had been even, until Sam scored that perfect goal it seemed. I didn't really think about anything else other than getting up to begin shouting and clapping.

It seemed he caught sight of me then as the third intermission buzz went off. Without even missing a beat, I left my seat to rush down to one of the side rink doors as Sam skated towards it. One of the rink marshals opened it as we both reached it at the same time. He dropped his hockey stick and wrapped one strong arm around my waist, lifting me up into a tight embrace.

I didn't care that there were hundreds of people watching or that there were many cameras flashing and clicking around us as he hugged me tightly. My arms wrapped around his neck as I buried my face into his shoulder.

"How are you even here right now?!"

He shouted over the crowd as he lowered me down. The

cold instantly biting into me as he let go of me. I became very aware of how much I wanted to be back in his arms.

"And don't you look hot in my number."

He winked with a coy smile. If it wasn't for the many people watching us, I would have kissed him as my emotions were running high.

"Katelyn thought it would be a nice surprise for you."

"It's a very nice surprise. I'm sorry I didn't come back to town after the hotel."

"Don't worry about that, you just go back in there and win this game. We can talk about it later."

"We will be celebrating later that's for sure."

Taking a hold of my hand, he kissed it gently before turning on his skates. My eyes were glued to his back as he headed across the rink to the entrance of the changing rooms. His team was waiting on the sidelines, all shouting and wolf whistling at him as he joined them.

My heart skipped a beat as the heat in me rose. What did he mean by celebrating? I let my mind wander a little wondering if that meant we were going to celebrate just the two of us or did that mean I'd be meeting the rest of his team. Either way, I felt strangely relaxed now I was near him.

I didn't realize how much I did miss him until he was holding me.

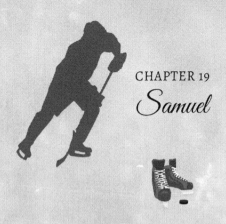

CHAPTER 19
Samuel

Once we scored the final goal for the night, 10-18, I couldn't wait to get out of my gear and find Kim. I knew she'd be with Katelyn and the others, but I just wanted her all to myself. We could hopefully talk, clear the air, and spend some time together.

And yet, the boys had other ideas. They wanted to party, celebrate my return and even the other team wanted to join. The match was friendly, no foul play and it reminded me of how much I love hockey.

Stepping out back into the rink once most of the crowd had emptied out, I saw a group was waiting for the team. James's wife and some of the other girls the boys would hang with were all waiting. Including Stacey, someone I had a fling with many times over the years. She made somewhat good company when the nights got lonely, but now all I saw was Kim.

God, she looked gorgeous in my jersey and if she wanted to wear only that later on tonight... I wouldn't say no. I wouldn't be able to control myself. She hadn't left my thoughts during the weeks apart.

I hadn't realized how buried my feelings were for her. Old ones I had forgotten about. Love wasn't much when you were a teen. My mom would often throw it in my face calling it puppy love, and that I would get bored of her.

One of the reasons I had ignored mom's calls and texts was that she would ask a million questions about me, about Kim and how it even happened.

"You joining us for a drink, Sam?"

Louis asked as he hooked an arm over one of the girls and Stacey caught my eyeline, smiling sweetly at me. Ignoring her, it felt like she didn't exist, because all I could do was look for Kim. Who had disappeared on me. "Nah, not tonight bud, I've got a girl to see."

Stacey's face dropped as she huffed and turned suddenly aiming for the door. Some part of me wanted to run after her, to explain it wasn't hard feelings or anything, but I wanted Kim.

I wanted her body against mine. I wanted her scent all over me. Her hands roaming free. I didn't want anyone else.

I had fallen. And hard. This new chapter of our lives would be different. We were grown, we had both been hurt and gone through the wars. I wanted to go through so much more with her at my side. As long as she'd have me.

As I looked around trying to see if she had left with Katelyn, I was grateful when my phone buzzed, and her name popped up.

> Went outside for some air. Want to go for a walk?

A walk sounded pretty good, it meant we could not only clear the air, but it also meant we would be alone, well kind of alone as I was sure some photographers might follow us. Hopefully we'd lose them though. Rushing to the main entrance as the last part of the crowd was leaving, they spotted me, all cheering and shouting. Not one to be rude, I couldn't get past them without getting a few photographs in and signing some shirts. Thankfully, someone had a pen as I never carried one. Everyone was in happy spirits, I'd felt rude if I ignored them and pushed my way through. Even if I was impatient to get away, I couldn't wait to see her.

Finally, I pushed open the doors and there she was, standing near the edge by the parking lot. Cars beeped as patrons unlocked their vehicles. Some were in lines already, while parking attendants helped direct the crowd out. Even with all the noise and lights, I was blind sided by Kimberly.

"There you are, I've been looking everywhere for you." She turned around as I walked towards her, her smile as bright and beautiful as ever. "I was beginning to think I'd stand out here all night."

She had a black puffer jacket wrapped around her as the winter chill had started to set in and winters in Quebec were cold. Although the sun had set hours ago, the sky had a pink purplish shade to it. Which usually only meant one thing, snow.

"I wouldn't leave you standing out here on your own."

Holding out my hand, I prayed she'd take it and when she did, I swear I turned into a little boy with a schoolboy crush. Linking her arm through mine, we headed to wherever our legs would take us.

Heading into the main city, we looked at the Christmas and fairy lights decorating the streets. The streets were a bustle filled with Christmas music, small market stalls of people selling ceramic decorations, glass, and woodwork as well as other bits and bobs.

Kim took her time looking at each stall while still holding onto my arm. With each move she made, I was glued to her side. I'd happily walk into traffic if that's what she wanted to do.

"Would you like any help, my dears?"

An older woman, at the handmade Christmas decorations stall, smiled up at Kim as she picked up a felt made dog that looked like Daisy. She examined it before putting it down, as if she had changed her mind.

"Buy it if you like it."

"You don't think it's silly?"

"I think it will be silly if you leave it and regret it later."

Jane used to do that. She'd see something she liked in the store and no matter how much she wanted it; she'd never buy it. One of my regrets was I didn't get to spoil her and gift her with the things I knew she deeply loved.

"If you don't buy it, I will buy it for you."

Rolling her eyes at me, Kim picked the dog back up and headed towards the till. Kim tapped her phone onto the card machine as the older woman wrapped the decoration up in tissue paper and popped it into a paper bag. A smile creeped across Kim's face as she swung the bag and did a little dance of excitement.

I had never seen her do that before and it made me wonder if she was letting her guard down a bit more with me. I hoped so.

As we continued on our walk, we came to a hot chocolate and warm apple cider stand with some seating outside. Thankfully, they were all under heat lamps. I ordered us both a hot chocolate, mine special with a shot of whiskey as I needed some liquid courage. Kim was making me nervous, she appeared more relaxed, more open and I wasn't sure why.

I was waiting for the other shoe to drop after I had disappeared for the last three weeks, and we hadn't really brought the subject up. Which meant, I was going to have to.

"Kim, I'm sorry I didn't come back to town after that morning in the hotel. Paula had me run ragged doing every interview possible, then we had to get the ball rolling with the charity match. I did try and take a day to travel up, but then Chris got me back into training and time just ran away."

At the end of my word vomit spew, I winced inwardly. She had just sat there listening to my every word as she cupped her hot chocolate mug in her hands, keeping them warm. Under the heat lamp, her skin glowed a warm flush. I couldn't help, but notice how her eyes sparkled with the fairy lights.

"Sam, I watched the interviews. Don't worry, I know you were busy, and I didn't want to keep distracting you by texting too much."

"You didn't need to text me to distract me."

A blush flashed along her cheeks as she took a sip of her drink. She had distracted me, even without hearing her voice or reading her words. Her image was imprinted in my brain and all I wanted to do was be next to her, or any way she wanted me.

"Shall we go back to the hotel after this?" she asked.

Her question took me by surprise as I thought we would be out for at least another hour. A quick glance around told me the market stalls were beginning to shut down for the night. I looked at my watch and saw it was getting close to eleven at night. Which was late, but it also meant the temperature was going to drop even more. I guessed we were both cold almost to our bones now. Feeling grateful the whiskey helped warm me up a little, I wondered if she was too cold.

Taking a sip of my drink, some small dab of whipped cream pressed against my nose. Kim had to hold back her laugh as she watched me make a mess of myself. Before I could even clean it off, she whipped out her phone and took a snap of me.

"OI! You're not going to sell that to some trashy magazines now, are you?"

"Why not? Bet I could make some decent money." She teased me, handing me a napkin.

"And to answer your question, yes, let's head back to the hotel."

IT WOULD HAVE TAKEN a while to walk back to the hotel, so I opted for us to grab a cab. The driver was only too excited to have me as a passenger. He badgered me into answering lots of questions and to sign a piece of paper for his son. Kim didn't seem annoyed or remotely bothered as she looked out the window watching the world go on by.

After we pulled up to the hotel and I paid the cab driver, we headed inside and surprisingly it was quiet. I assumed that the boys and the other team may have gone into town to celebrate. Or they were already in bed, most likely celebrating with their chosen partners.

Heading upstairs to the the floor, I assumed her room was on, Kim stayed quiet. When we reached her door, we both stopped outside of it. I wasn't sure where we were going next, did she want me to join her? Or would it be better for both of us if I left to head back to my room, where me and my hand would become best friends?

"It was nice spending time with you."

"Yeah, I've missed that face of yours."

Why was I so nervous? It wasn't as if I hadn't recently had this girl pressed up against me. Granted we always had clothes on, but I could let my imagination think otherwise. She lowered her eyes from me, biting her bottom lip and all I could think about was biting it myself.

"Well, goodnight then."

She leaned forward a little then leaned back, turning towards her room door. I wasn't sure what to do other than grabbing her wrist and pulling her back round.

As I pulled her into me, she wrapped her arms around me hugging me tightly as I hugged her back. My palms felt slightly sweaty as I thought about making the next move, I didn't want to push. Only go at her pace. Whatever that was.

Looking up at me, her long lashes made me crave her more and without thinking, I lifted her chin up a little and brushed my lips against hers. Feeling her melt almost into me, I kept kissing her. Softly and with care at first as my hand went round and cupped the back of her neck while my other hand rested on the base of her back.

She tasted a little of chocolate and as I deepened our kiss, we moved backwards until her back landed on the hotel room door. Her hands wrapped themselves up in my hair, pulling me closer to her.

Seconds later, one hand left my hair then the beep of the door went as she held the room card up to unlock it. We almost fell into the room, paying more attention to one another than the door opening. Barely keeping ourselves up right, we moved out of the doorway, letting it shut behind us. I couldn't contain my hunger for her as I lifted her up, her legs wrapping around my waist.

Slamming her against the wall that connected the room and the bathroom, I left her lips as I trailed kisses down her neck. She let out a soft moan, which only drove my desires higher.

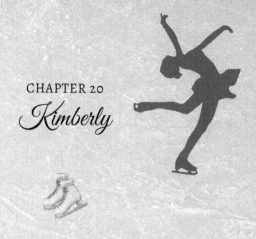

His mouth left mine and he began to kiss tenderly with a slight firmness against my neck. I let out a small moan, my body enjoying his touch. His strong arms held tightly on my thighs as my legs remained locked around his waist. I had thought about this moment all night. After watching him play and when he lifted me up for a hug, I couldn't wait to really wrap my legs around him.

Nipping at my ear lobe as he pushed harder into me, I ran my hands into his hair, over his neck, his shoulders, anywhere I could. I wanted all of him and I was going to get it.

My heartbeat raced in my ears as the heat grew inside of me. I couldn't get over how broad his shoulders were. When we were teens and fooled around, he was scrawny and barely had any muscle to him and now, I couldn't wait to get his clothes off.

Tearing at his waistline, I found his shirt and began to pull it off. I could feel his laughter against my skin as he stopped kissing me. Bringing his face to meet mine, his eyes held so much hunger and wanting. I had never been looked at that way before, even when I was married.

Luke would always take great care to be extra gentle. He wasn't adventurous and sometimes I just wanted to be ravished. Being the gentle soul he was, he could never bring himself to do it. Yet, Sam was looking at me as if I were the last person on the planet and he had to have me.

"Are you sure this is what you want?"

He stopped. Why had he stopped? Looking at him again, his green eyes softened, and I noticed the slight brown specks inside them. I had forgotten how beautiful his eyes were. Cupping his face, I kissed him gently, welcoming, and as I pulled away, I could feel his smile on his lips against mine.

"Sam, I have wanted this – Needed this for a long time."

He took that as his sign that the gloves were off, I was all his and I didn't need to hint or say anything else. He just knew what to do. Holding me still, we walked towards the bed and as he sat down, I kept my legs around his waist and began kissing him with a kind of need I had forgotten about.

Feeling his arousal against my thigh, my own heat flashed, causing my body to ache for his. I wanted him. Desired him. Needed him. Pushing myself up a bit, he groaned at the fabric between us that kept us apart, but it didn't stop me as I grinded against him. Nipping at his bottom lip and kissing him harder than before, our tongues joining once again, I swear I heard him growl. "If you – keep rubbing against me like that – I will ruin all the fun before it starts."

He breathlessly got out between my kisses, and I couldn't help but laugh a little. It had been so long since I had felt the touch of another human being. I was grateful it would be him and not some total stranger I met at a bar. This was someone who had taken my virginity as well as my heart.

"Well then, you best calm yourself down. We are in for a long night."

He groaned more as he rolled his eyes. Clearly I had said the right thing as seconds later he was grabbing the back of my neck, and practically slammed his lips against mine. His other hand was running freely underneath my clothes, touching my bare skin. I had opted for no bra tonight, more so to be comfortable, but as his fingers found my breast, I let out a content sigh. I had made a great choice with no bra.

Just as he had done before, he began rubbing against my nipple with his thumb, only lightly enough to get me moaning a little. He knew what he was doing, and I was happy to let him explore.

Tearing at his shirt once again, I pulled away slightly as I lifted his shirt up and over his head, exposing his beautiful chest. I took notice of the small, faded scars here and there. Some still a little red and others from injuries long past. Trailing my fingers down one near his neck, I couldn't help but think they were a beautiful contrast against his golden kissed skin.

"Where's this one from?"

"Glass bottle to the throat. Luckily, he missed and caught my shoulder instead."

"I don't really count that as lucky. What about this one?"

Another scar ran down his right bicep to his elbow.

"Fight with a hockey skate blade. Most of these are from hockey games."

"Are any from..." I bit my lip. I didn't want to ask and change the mood, but I saw him realize what I was going to ask.

"No, none of them are from him."

A small smile fell to my lips as he leaned in, brushing his lips against mine. He kissed me lightly and ran his hands up my thighs. Shivering in response as his lips met mine and again, he trailed his lips down to my jawline, to my neck and I arched my back in response. My need for him grew as a pulsing started between my legs. I ached more for him, desperately wishing he would just take my clothes off and have his way with me.

Almost as if he read my mind, he lifted the jersey over my head then the long-sleeved t-shirt. Leaving my breasts completely exposed, a soft flush rushed to my skin as a low rumble rose from his throat as he looked down at me.

He leaned in and as I arched my back, he lowered his mouth to one of my nipples and began licking and nipping while his hand was on the other one. The sudden change in temperature sent shivers to run down my spine as my core became wet, desperate to have all of him.

His hand dropped my breast and ran down my side, to my waist then began moving towards my center. My body cried out for more. I ached for him to touch me. And as his hand pressed against the fabric that separated us, I could feel him smile against my breast.

"You feel ready for me, good girl."

His voice sounded husky and happy. He knew what he was doing to me, without even really trying. It had been way too long since someone touched me the way he was touching me. As he rubbed the palm of his hand up and down, it got me more riled up. I couldn't help but move in return, desperate for a real touch. Lifting myself up slightly off his lap, I gave him more access.

Riding the waves of his movements and the feelings that were coming out of me, I couldn't control my moans. When his hand suddenly left me, I felt that sudden loss and cold. He didn't wait long until he was running his hand over my waist-line and pushing his hand inside.

"Take them off," I commanded breathlessly.

"With pleasure."

Lifting me up, he flipped me, so my back now rested on the bed, and he yanked my jeans off. Sam tossed my jeans across the room, before unbuttoning and pushing his own off his body. Exposing himself even more, his erection demanded to be released from his boxers.

My breath caught in my throat as he lifted me up again, his arm slipping around my waist. Once he lifted me further up the bed, his lips again started moving from my collarbone and down my body. He was kissing everywhere while his hands continued to explore.

Pulling my black panties down, I thanked myself for packing some sexy ones. Sam kissed around my navel and hip bones then his palm was back between my legs. Looking down at him, I saw a smile slide across his face then finally he slid a finger inside me. I let out a moan as he watched me.

His movements were gentle at first, getting the feel of me and watching me closely to see what I liked. In and out. He slid another finger inside and his thumb began rubbing my clit in circular motions. Gripping some of the bedsheet with one hand, the other pulling lightly at his hair. He moaned in return as I lifted a leg up to wrap around his waist.

"Please," I uttered.

I wanted him. I needed him inside me. I had never been able to come with foreplay and now this was the ultimate torture. I needed his dick inside me. Now. Slowing his pace, he withdrew his fingers and left me. Standing on the edge of the bed, he stared down at me, looking at every inch of me.

"Do you have any condoms?"

My eyes widened a little as I thought about it. I hadn't packed any, it wasn't something I'd think about. I didn't really think this would have been happening either and he laughed a little.

"Well, I best run up to my room to go grab some then. While you wait here, don't move. I will be back."

Pulling his jeans and t-shirt back on as well as his sneakers. He left me seconds later, lying completely naked and waiting for him.

CHAPTER 21
Samuel

I had never rushed up a set of stairs as fast as this before, in my life. I had given up waiting for the elevator as I wanted to rush back to Kimberly. I needed to rush back to her. Thankfully I have managed to squeeze my erection back in my pants, even if it was a little painful. I prayed I didn't bump into anyone as I reached my room and almost pushed the door off the hinges as I charged in.

Condoms, condoms, I know I packed a few.

I always packed them every trip because even if I didn't need one, one of the boys nine times out of ten needed one. The clock was ticking if I took too long. Kim might change her mind and not be interested anymore. We needed to ride this high, and I wanted her to ride me.

As my phone buzzed while still hunting, going through every drawer, bag, and suitcase I had shoved into this tiny room, I groaned before pulling the phone out and seeing it was a text from Kim. Yep, she had changed her mind.

Hesitating to open it, I stopped for a second, my hype and mood slowly disappearing until I opened the message and there in all her splendor was a naked selfie and the words 'I'm waiting'.

As my blood rushed back down to my cock, I looked even harder before realizing that I wasn't thinking. I had put the pack of condoms in the bathroom. In a logical place.

Sprinting back downstairs, I was out of breath by the time I reached Kim's room door and before I had a chance to even knock, she opened it slightly, poking her head around the crack.

"Yes, may I help you?" she teased.

I just wanted to push open the door and take her, but I had to play along it seemed before she would let me in.

"I'm room service."

"Have you come to service the room or something else?"

Leaning in closer to the door, my eyes darkened as I wet my lips a little and she looked up at me playfully.

"If you don't open this door, I will just have to drag you out and fuck you in the hallway."

Laughing a little, she opened the door just enough to allow me to step in. Before even a breath had passed, I had her pulled up against me, still completely naked. Kim didn't waste any time as her hands went to my jeans button, popped it and off they came.

I couldn't get my shoes off quick enough as I did that funny walk with my jeans hooked on my ankles as she walked backwards towards the bed. Her hand plunged down my boxers and started rubbing my cock, which thankfully had returned to its standing salute.

Her motions caused me to shudder slightly as she went at a slow, teasing pace. My hand found her core again, diving a finger deep inside and as she arched backwards, her back met the bed, thankfully.

We fell together and a small laugh erupted from her as I

kissed her deeply. I wanted to make her mine, only mine. Letting go of my cock, she pulled my t-shirt back over my head then pushed my boxers down. Once I kicked off the fabric ankle cuffs, I was just as naked as she was. Her beautiful creamy skin felt soft to the touch and smelt of fresh lemons and the smell of after it rains.

Breaking the kiss, I looked down at her.

God, she was beautiful.

My fingers still gently played with her, teasing her, and brought her to the edge as her eyes rolled back in her head. She bit down on her bottom lip and she moaned delightfully, enjoying herself.

Removing myself completely from her, she moaned in protest as I fished the condoms out from my jeans pocket. I ripped one open and started to slide it down my cock. Which had been very well behaved and not ruining this reunion for both of us.

As I leaned back down, she spread her legs open and wrapped both of them around my legs, one a little further up on my thigh then the other. I guided myself in, she felt perfect, taking my dick like she was made for it. She melted in my arms, causing a deep moan to escape my lips.

Within moments she had her arms wrapped around my neck, pulling me closer to her as I devoured every inch of her. Kissing anywhere I could possibly reach. Her lips, her neck, her jaw, her breasts. I wanted all of her.

"Fuck me."

She breathlessly whispered in my ear, and I was happy to oblige as I picked up speed. Slamming deep inside her, she wrapped her legs tighter around me as she moved along with me. I brought her to the point she had been begging for and when that amazing sound floated from her lips, I continued. Bringing her to ecstasy again and again. Each time, her eyes rolled in the back of her head, her legs shook, but a smile looked up at me. Until finally I could no longer contain myself and my release finally came.

I didn't want to remove myself from her. I wanted to stay put as I kept myself up, not wanting to crush her with my weight. She kissed me gently, lovingly on the lips and eventually we untangled ourselves from each other and I went to clean myself off.

"I could get used to that." She shouted as I stood in the bathroom.

"If you want to keep doing that, we can."

I replied and I meant it. I would continue to fall for her, in love with her and no matter how much I wanted to stop, it wasn't going to happen. She was slowly completing me.

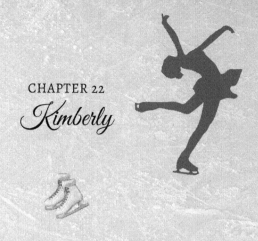

CHAPTER 22
Kimberly

L ying next to each other, naked and embraced, I felt safe. Relaxed and the feeling of grief was in the back of my mind. I was here, in this moment and not someone in the dark, alone and lost.

Sam ran his fingers through my hair as he hugged me tightly half awake, the blanket only covering our bottom half. He was a walking hot water bottle and kept me warm. With a smile against my lips and a feeling of complete and utter bliss, I felt my eyes slowly close and then open again as he shifted, getting more comfortable.

"We should get some sleep."

Sam just made a hmm noise as I looked up at him, his eyes still closed, and his arm tightened around my shoulders. I didn't think I'd be able to fall asleep like this but when the sun broke through the curtains and Sam began to stir, I realized it was morning.

As he slipped out of bed slowly, leaving me wrapped up in blankets, he kissed the top of my head and a few minutes later the shower began to run. Sleepily, I woke myself up and I most certainly wasn't ready for this night to end.

"You weren't allowed to leave me."

I said leaning against the doorframe. He looked even hotter with his messed-up sex hair and covered in soap suds. Without him even objecting, I joined him in the shower and began washing him. First his arms, then his chest and as I moved my hands slowly down his body, he breathed out a deep sigh.

Until I found his erection, ready and waiting. Rubbing up and down with soap covered hands, I began to clean him, and he threw his head back a little, moaning lightly as I picked up the speed. Once all the soap was off and it was just water running down our bodies, I got down on my knees and began kissing his thighs, making my way back up until I started kissing the tip of his dick and then wrapped my mouth around it.

He moaned even deeper as one of his hands found my hair, tangling his fingers as I moved my head back and forth, licking, sucking, and biting the tip gently. His moans became louder as he moved himself back and forth, joining me and I felt the hot sensation hit the back of my throat and the salty taste of his orgasm, swallowing it.

Pulling me up then suddenly, his lips found mine as he kissed me passionately. Tasting himself against my lips didn't seem to bother him as his fingers ran down my back, desperately trying to find any part of me he could grab.

"You are – amazing."

His voice husky against my lips as he nipped the bottom lip, pulling at it gently.

"I want to give you one now."

He said as his hands moved down and found my center, again ready and waiting for him and as he slid a finger in, I felt my body shudder at his touch. Moving in and out at a mixture pace, sometimes slow and sometimes a little fast. He popped in another finger and within minutes there were three there and his thumb rubbed against my clit.

"Oh God."

It's all I could say as I lifted a leg and he held it closely, giving him more access to me and I felt his erection suddenly return. I had never known a man to get turned on so quickly after finishing and yet there he was, standing and ready.

"I want you."

I said looking down at him as my eyes darkened as he continued to play with me, bringing me closer to the edge than ever before.

"Not yet."

He breathed against my neck as he kissed it. We needed to be safe, of course, but right now I didn't care. I wanted him inside me again, ruining me, claiming me as his own.

"Don't tease me."

I practically begged as his fingers slowed.

"Kimmy, I wanna fuck you until you can't walk. I wanna hear you scream my name out. I want to make you completely mine."

He growled and whispered in my ear as he pulled his fingers out and I grabbed a hold of his cock, pulling him slightly towards me. It teased at my entrance, as the warm water brushed against our skin. I knew he was saying not yet because we had no condoms in here with us, but I didn't care. I craved him.

"We need to be sensible, sadly, my little skater."

Kissing me deeply, he pulled away seconds later and began lathering up some soap in his hands and started to wash me from head to toe. Tenderly and with every touch my body screamed for him even more.

I wanted out of this shower more than anything. The condoms were left on the bedside table and without saying a word and still covered in soap, I hopped out of the shower and rushed to grab one. His laughter rang from the bathroom as I appeared seconds later, opening the packet and began sliding it down his cock.

"Eager, are we?"

He joked as he groaned at my touch and I didn't say a word, just hooked my leg around his waist again and kissed him. My tongue teased his lips as he parted them and joined mine pulling me closer to him.

His cock finally took hold of me, and I completely lost myself in him. Lifting me up and pinning me against the shower wall, the coldness of the tile took my breath away slightly. I didn't have time to really think about it though as he started pounding into me. Quick movements, his mouth breaking from me and kissing my neck as one hand pinned mine against the wall.

I couldn't think.

I couldn't breathe.

I was wrapped up in him.

Only him.

And I loved every second of it.

As I came to my end, he joined me seconds later and I collapsed against him, unable to feel my legs or move. A chuckle from his chest rumbled as he let me down gently. My head was spinning, and my legs were wobblily. I was spent.

"I guess we need to wash again."

He joked as he got out of the shower and cleaned himself up. Wrapping a towel around himself, he smiled at me and left me to shower. Or attempt to shower as my hands were shaking.

I COULD HAVE EASILY SPENT the rest of my days in that hotel room as we ordered room service, had multiple sexual sessions, enjoyed each other's company, and really got to know one another. However, reality set in as I stood at the gate as my plane called passengers to board.

Katelyn was under the strictest of orders by Sam to keep me company, as he had been called into a few emergency things, I didn't ask what. But he ordered Katelyn to stuck by me all the way to my front door as he held tightly on to my hand, desperate not to let go.

"I will see you on Friday." I assured him as I kissed him lightly on the cheek.

"I'm sorry I can't come with you as planned. You'd think, I wouldn't be needed as much as I have been lately. And Friday is so far away."

He sounded like a child who was ready to have a tantrum and I rolled my eyes at him. Friday did seem a long time away, but I knew as soon as my feet landed on the ground, I would be in wedding planner mode.

Joseph and Beth had already texted me multiple times over the weekend asking where this was, when was this coming, and so many more wedding related questions. I knew I'd get the third degree when I arrived home as mom was still not speaking to me.

The only ones who seemed remotely happy with Sam and I kinda seeing each other. Or are we together now? I wasn't too sure on the technicalities of everything, the girls group chat hadn't stopped messaging. Especially when I sent a photograph of a topless Sam lying in bed, they nearly lost their shit.

"Friday will arrive before we know it. We both have a busy week planned and don't forget," leaning up on my toes to whisper in his ear, "I have a very pretty dress that I will need help getting out of."

His smile grew as he hugged me tightly, nuzzling his head into my neck and I swore if he hugged me any tighter, he would break something.

"Come on lovebirds." Shouted Katelyn as she headed through the gate.

Flashes of cameras came from the waiting room as some photographers had followed us from the hotel, Sam let go of me and as much as I wanted him to kiss me goodbye, I knew he wouldn't. We already discussed public displays and keeping them at the minimum was for the best.

"I will see you back home."

His sheepish smile was the last thing I saw as I went through the gate and boarded the plane. He would be kept busy this week as Katelyn and Paula had already told him he had multiple interviews lined up and when he arrived Friday, the charity game would need discussing.

They had arranged the game to be just after Christmas but before New year's. During that odd week everyone had post-Christmas where you didn't know what day or time it even was. It was a good idea to do it then, it meant the town would be busy, we'd have lots of footfall and it gave everyone something to do.

Before I turned my phone off, it buzzed just as the plane began taxiing and Sam's name flashed up, his words leaving me with a blush and a small smile.

Miss those lips already. See you soon my little skater.

I hadn't realized until he called me that in the shower that was the nickname he gave me back in high school. I most certainly was his little skater and always would be.

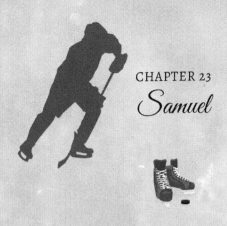

Hitting the gym was the last thing I wanted to do after all the workouts over the weekend with Kim. Yet here I was, running the treadmill as it was leg day. Already I was feeling ready to fall over as my legs went jelly like. Louis sat on the bench next to me pulling weights, Jason was on the bench-press, with Duncan spotting for him, James was working on some cardio and Ryan was going fast and hard on the rowing machine.

No one said a word.

No one asked me questions.

Louis, I could see, was desperate for me to spill the tea on why I didn't answer any calls or texts, why I hadn't gone training the following day and why Chris was making me do more work today as punishment.

The music blasted through our gym speakers loudly and helped drown out any thoughts I had of Kim. Imagining her body pressed up against mine, her mouth around my cock. Shaking my head as the thoughts came, I began to run a little faster, picking up speed until they disappeared.

"So, you're really not gonna tell us what happened then over the weekend?" Jason asked as he did his last rep.

"Nothing to tell."

"Bullshit, and you know it. You didn't even answer Paula and we all know she doesn't like being ignored." Jason stood from the bench and patted himself dry with his towel. The others stopped their workouts to listen in.

"Ah ha, yeah, I haven't heard the end of that, trust me."

"Seriously though bro, what happened? Can you at least tell us you got some."

Ryan annoyingly smiled as he pretended to hump the air. He still had that immature frat boy energy. At some point, I had been just like him. Back before I realized I couldn't carry on screwing myself through a never ending line of women and wanted to settle down one day.

Maybe I could settle down with Kim if she wanted to.

"Yeah. I got some and plenty more after that."

"WHAYYY!!"

All the guys, well aside from Duncan as he very rarely made a peep, all cheered sarcastically as if I were a virgin who had just lost his V card. Shaking my head and laughing them off, I headed to the changing rooms. Like a group of teenage girls, they followed, all still eager to learn more.

I was finally able to hit the showers then get ready shortly afterwards. I eagerly waited for the text from Kim to say she had got home safely, which wouldn't be for another few hours. Paula had already called me to say I had a talk show this afternoon. This interview was to promote the charity event, and to announce the teams that will be joining.

We had secured ten hockey teams and many multimillion-dollar companions who had offered to sponsor the young hockey players and ice skaters. We had got lucky with a few of them, mostly businesses looking to advertise their brand on uniforms.

Olivia, the newscaster, had also told Paula and the others the special feature her channel had been working on would be going live this Wednesday. I looked forward to seeing it, knowing it featured Kim.

"Once you're done Sam, wanna hit a bar for a few?" Jason asked, looking rather hopeful.

"Maybe dude, will text you."

Honestly, a few drinks with the boys would help clear my head and help break up the days as Friday was going to take a long time to arrive, unless I kept myself busy.

WEDNESDAY EVENING.

> Joe and I are going out drinking tonight, a late stag kinda thing, few of his army buddies are coming as well.

Kim and I had been back and forth texting all day as she finished up her brother's wedding things as well as working back at the rink getting her girls prepped for their competition.

Each day so far had been filled with gym, tv appearances, meeting up with the boys then sitting at my apartment flicking through the television channels, waiting for Kim to message me back.

I didn't realize how crappy and routine my life had become until I was back sitting on my couch. I didn't even have a dog around to keep me company. Katelyn had opted to stay with Kim as she had bits to do with the charity event and Kim had been kind enough to let her sleep in the guest bedroom of her house.

From the outside, her house seemed huge, and I had to stop myself many times from asking what Luke did for them to own a home like that. I didn't really like talking about him, the memory of him made Kim sad. Even though I knew we both moved on previously and had a past, it made me a little jealous he had spent so many years with her.

Whereas my stupidity and cowards made me lose out. I would make up for it one way or another.

> Army buddies?

>> Don't worry about them honestly, I used to babysit one of them and the others are all married. Joe is the last one to get hitched, so they had to come.'

> Oh, I'm not worried, I know you'd kick some guys ass if he tried anything.

> I feel sorry for the guys having to keep up with you.

>> It will be a fun night. Joe is excited. He can't wait to marry Beth, he has been at mine all day.

>> He's asked me a lot of questions about you. Mom started speaking to me today as well, she's still mad you haven't been round for dinner before the wedding.

I had forgotten I had agreed to have dinner with Kim's family before the wedding, it was the right thing to do and now the wedding was going to be here on Saturday. As the conversation went quiet, more so on my end as I had an idea and one, I hoped I'd be able to work. Looking for Paula's number, it took a few rings before she finally answered me and didn't seem at all impressed by the late call.

"What? It's late."

"Sorry, eh, any chance we can push tomorrow's meetings and we maybe move them to next week."

"And why should we do that?"

"Well, eh, as we speak, I've rebooked my flight back to Merrifort a day early."

I pulled my phone back from my ear and waited for the eruption of shouting and screaming that I was used to from Paula. There wasn't any. She was quiet for once. Maybe preparing to boil.

"Alright, I had a feeling you were going to do this anyway, so I moved the meetings already. What time is your flight?"

"Okay, where is Paula and what have you done with her?"

I was surprised how she didn't question me. Normally I was used to her telling me where I was going, and what I was doing. She would pretty much plan my entire life month by month. She hated rain checking or changing things.

"I'm not your mother, Sam. You can go and do as you please. Katelyn had already asked for me to come a day early and I assumed if I was going early, you'd want to come too. Clearly, I was right."

"You do know me the best."

I tried to cover my sudden happiness as I got up off the couch and headed to pack. If I could make it happen, I would be staying longer than a few days this time. Meetings, news reports and everything else had to wait. I already missed many years away from Kim and I didn't want to miss anymore.

She was suddenly becoming the most important person in

my life. As much as I hated myself for admitting it, I was falling in love with her.

Fast and unexpected.

I had always been in love with her, puppy love as teens and now a mature healthy adult love. Now, I saw her for who she had become, and I wasn't going to lose her.

C hucking my house keys on the sideboard and kicking off my shoes, I was so happy to be home. The snow was starting to fall already, earlier than normal and the drive back and forth to the rink was colder than usual. I couldn't wait to curl up on the couch with a glass of wine. Daisy would cuddle up next to me and we would watch some crappy television.

Katelyn had mentioned Matthew, the other part of the team was flying in this morning, and she left to pick him up at the airport. Thankfully, she said she was going to stay at the local B&B with him as I wouldn't have had the room for another person.

I didn't ask questions, but she mentioned they have always had a thing for each other and sometimes they would end up in bed together. Neither of them wanted a relationship, so it worked out perfectly.

The girls didn't seem too happy when I made them meet me at seven in the morning. They weren't off school yet, so an hour each morning before their classes wouldn't kill them. If anything, it sets them up for the day. Or at least that's what my coach used to say.

I contemplated going back to bed, the clock showed ten in the morning. Daisy seemed annoyed she had been woken up when I came home and took herself to bed. I was left without much company in the end.

Checking my phone, I noticed I hadn't heard from Sam yet and usually I would have by now. Perhaps he was sleeping in or had an even earlier morning than me. My head hurt a little from last night's drinking session with Joe and his army friends. I was glad when it reached midnight and they wanted to hit a strip club in the next town over as it gave me a reason to escape.

Joe, bless him, looked mortified at the thought. He begged me to stay, to rescue him. What kind of best woman would I be if I helped him out? Judging by the photograph Beth sent me when he got home, he was in a right drunken state and clearly had a great time.

> Hey! Haven't heard from you this morning, hope you're ok.

> One more sleep.

No reply, but the text bubble appeared green, so he wasn't anywhere where there wasn't a signal, or had his phone off. I tried not to think much into it, I had never been that girl who worried where the guy she was speaking to was at 24/7.

Instead of falling asleep, I opted to take Daisy out for a walk. It may have been a little cold, but it was nothing our warm coats wouldn't fix. Wrapping her up in her hot pink fleece dog coat and popping a beanie over her head. She may have been a fluffy dog, but she always felt the cold more than other dogs her breed.

"Don't worry babes, we will only be out for twenty minutes, tops. You haven't had a walk in a few days so now we are having one."

She nuzzled her nose into my hand as I shrugged on my warm coat and tugged on my hat. One thing I hated the most was cold ears. Making sure we had everything for our walk as I hated getting caught out with no bags to clean up any mess, we headed out the door.

And smacked into another person. Daisy barked protectively as I squealed as the person frightened me. Big strong arms held me up as Daisy cowered behind me still barking. Some great guard dog she was.

"Hi, Kimmy."

Samuel. It took me a second to realize it was him and as soon as I did my arms were around his neck as I hugged him tightly. This was indeed a surprise as I was half expecting him to show up late tomorrow. He embraced me back and Daisy stopped her barking almost instantly, sniffing around at our feet.

"You don't mind me showing up like this do you?"

"Of course not! I'm happy to see you."

Kissing him gently on the lips, I felt this overwhelming feeling of happiness. We stood there on my front porch with the snow falling slowly around us. I would have easily invited him inside, but I was very aware of Daisy as she nudged me a little, making sure I didn't forget her.

"I'm taking Daisy for a walk. You're welcome to join or you can stay here and keep warm, I won't be long."

He stood there with his hands on my waist, looking at me then at Daisy, clearly trying to decide what would be the best option for him. I wouldn't have blamed him if he didn't want to go for a walk. He looked like he needed some sleep, traveling really knocked it out of you sometimes and it would be mean of me if I expected him to use up what little energy he had left on me.

"Tell you what, I will go for this walk, you go inside, get yourself cozy by the fire, or grab a shower and then tuck yourself up in bed. I won't be long I promise."

"Honestly, that sounds perfect, but only as long as you're sure. I don't mind."

"Sam, you look like death warmed up. Go and rest."

He looked relieved as I decided for him, kissing him lightly on the cheek. He picked up his suitcase and headed inside as Daisy and I took our much-needed walk around the block. As soon as we were far enough away, I called Crystal to tell her Sam was here.

"Are you seriously telling me right now that Samuel Jones, the Captain of the Vancouver Devils, man of the hour just showed up at your doorstep a day early?!"

"You're really setting the bar low there, Crys. I think I'm going to take him round mom's tonight. Joe needs me to go over some last-minute wedding details and well, they keep complaining they haven't met Sam."

"Well, they have met him, just not the new him."

Crystal tutted on the other end of the phone, and I could picture the attitude she expressed. I could hear Lacy trying to quietly whisper in the background. I just knew she was asking a question about me or had something to say about my idea. They had started spending a lot more time at Crystal's apartment. I was waiting for them to share that they had moved in together.

"Do you think that's wise Kim? Your mom might flip out." Lacy had apparently taken over the phone call. "Sorry, Crys put you on speaker."

"It's not wise, it's ballsy and not like Kim at all. I think this hockey player's dick has gone straight to her head."

Crystal chimed in and I had to hold back my laughter. Daisy tugged on her leash as we rounded the corner of Elm Street, three blocks away from our home. I hadn't realized how far we had walked, I had been distracted by my phone call. The snow was getting heavier.

"I'm gonna head back home, girls. The weather is getting pretty bad, and I'd rather not slip and die in the snow."

"Not before you get some extra D."

Rolling my eyes at Crystal, I sighed. She spent far too much time with her brothers or listening to way too many fuckboy podcasts. Heading back home, the sky was fading into a beautiful pink shade as the snow continued to fall. It was so beautiful, and one of the main reasons I was happy Luke agreed to move here after we graduated.

I kicked my shoes off on the front porch before taking off Daisy's coat and beanie. She shook any snow that sat on her fur and quickly headed inside. No doubt to lie in front of the fire.

My clothes were a little wet, and I didn't want to sit around in them for too long. After heading upstairs, I stripped off in the bathroom. Hanging my trousers over the shower door and coat on the towel rack. The room was still a little steamy, Sam must have taken my advice and had a shower.

Which meant he probably climbed into my bed. I wanted to join him, cuddle up and get warm together. However, I threw on my bathrobe and headed back downstairs. I had a few emails to answer from the parents of my team. My stomach decided to take that moment to grumble, reminding me that I hadn't eaten since breakfast.

I was used to being an early riser, but after lunch, my eyes began going a little square. Daisy had headed upstairs after having her lunch and I had no doubt she was in the guest bedroom lying down on the bed.

Climbing into bed minutes later, I gave up trying to keep myself awake. I set my alarm for an hour and looked down at Sam who laid with his pillow tucked under his arm. Laying next to him, I felt my heart begin to race and the sudden panic rise.

Luke was the last man who slept in this bed with me.

And now, Sam was in his spot.

How easily I had replaced my husband with the next guy who showed me any affection. The feeling of betrayal and shame washed over me and seconds later I was sitting up crying. Sam quickly woke up wondering what the hell was going on.

"Kim – Kimmy – It's alright – What's the matter, babe?"

I couldn't get my words out. I couldn't breathe. The tightness on my chest was holding me firmly. I was a terrible woman. The town all looked at me with their judgmental eyes. It had only been just over a year and so easily I had forgotten Luke. I'd never forget him.

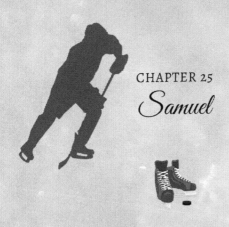

After Kim had left, I tried not to snoop too much around her house. I expected to find photographs and things that belonged to her previous husband, but I only came across a couple of photographs. One of them on her fireplace and the other on her vanity table.

One photograph of them at their wedding and another from their graduation ceremony. I couldn't remember if she mentioned they met in university. I didn't know much about her relationship; I was too afraid to ask.

Stealing her shower and changing into a fresh pair of boxers and joggers, I took full opportunity to get into bed, the sheets smelled of her and I instantly fell asleep. I did not however anticipate her waking me up to a flood of tears and in full blown panic mode.

It took me a few seconds to realize what was going on. I wasn't sure if I was meant to put my arms around her and hug her or leave her alone as she tried to calm herself down. I had seen her like this before, well almost like this. This seemed to be a lot worse than before.

"Kim, what can I do? Do you need me to go? Call someone?"

"No," she breathed, counting her breath, "Don't leave. I'm okay."

"You don't sound okay."

She didn't. And now I felt panic myself as I sat up fully and had her turn to face me, my hands bracing her shoulders.

"Count with me."

Counting five in, holding then counting five out, we breathed together. I had seen someone do something like this on a television show and thought maybe this might help. And remarkably it did. Something about breathing along with someone else, watching their chest rise and fall helps you regulate your breathing and slow your heart rate.

"I'm going to get you some water, I will be right back."

As fast as I could, I headed downstairs and got her a glass of water. Standing beside her side of the bed, I handed her the glass. Sitting down next to her as she took little sips, I watched her still holding her chest as if it hurt.

"Now, do you mind telling me what's wrong?"

We sat there in silence, the only real noise was Daisy whimpering as she appeared in the bedroom. She climbed up in bed with us, resting her head on Kim's lap before she buried her head in her lap.

"I, eh – you," she couldn't get her words out, still shaky. I was waiting for her to say she didn't want to see me anymore.

"It's just, Luke was the last man who slept in here and I feel like a terrible person for not mourning him more..."

Taking her hand in mine, I tried my best to reassure her. I only knew of death because of Jane. But losing a partner, I'm sure, was very different. I missed Jane less now as time had passed but I always thought about her. Kim had lost Luke just over a year ago. Moving on with your life, perhaps creating something new with someone had its benefits but also, guilt would show its ugly head.

"After Jane died, I was terrified to come back here. I didn't want to see anything that reminded me of her. I just stayed away, thinking that the grief would go away if I wasn't in a place that reminded me of her."

She looked at me with tear-stained eyes and redness in her cheeks.

"Coming back here, that first day, I almost turned my car around and left. But then, I saw you. And it reminded me that many things may change, but some things are constant. You have always been a constant," I paused for a breath. Checking to see if she still listened, I was trying my best to reassure her.

"Now, I don't know Luke or who you were when you were married. But this woman I know right now is stronger than ever before, confident, kind, funny and sexy to boot."

She laughed a little under her breath as she squeezed my hand. I wished she could see herself, the way I saw her. She took my breath away and no matter how much I continued to fight my head and my heart, they knew what I wanted, and I wanted her.

"From what I can see, you have mourned him, and you still do. You lost a piece of yourself when he died, and I think you are still trying to find it. But, you need to live without it. You have to accept that this is the new you. The person you were before and during Luke, is not here. Instead, there is someone who has faced pain, hurt and loss and came out the other side."

Cupping one of my cheeks, she smiled softly, through the tears that broke through and looked at me with ease in her eyes, possibly understanding.

"Since when did you become so wise?"

"Oh, I've always been wise, I just never wanted to show anyone my greatness."

"Greatness, huh?"

"I owe a lot of it to you, Kim. You have always believed in me, even after what I did. I would follow your story throughout the news, the articles, and watch your videos of you skating. When I heard about Luke, I desperately wanted to reach out...but thought it wouldn't have been the smartest thing to do."

She lowered her eyes from me, and her hand dropped. I wanted to hug her tightly then, to take away every pain, every hurt, all of it away from her and protect her from ever feeling those feelings again.

"I don't know what it's like to lose a husband, or a partner, but I know what it feels like to have your heart broken. And I hope, one day, I can help repair yours."

She choked back a cry and Daisy moved her head in her hand, trying to comfort her as well. They had a great bond, and I was grateful to the furball who helped soothe her.

"Shall we try and get some rest? Or would you like to go out somewhere? We can do whatever you feel like doing." I asked, concerned a little. She looked tired.

"Can you just hold me for a bit? And then we can go to my parents for dinner. I have to see Joe about some wedding things."

She still wanted me to meet her parents. I thought I would be more worried as I assumed they knew everything, but I wasn't worried. I would do anything that made her happy. Even if that did mean sitting there with her mom and dad as they judged me and possibly threatened me with guns.

"Sounds good to me."

As she moved herself up towards the top of the bed, I joined her as did Daisy, snuggling up against our feet.

Opening my arm out, Kim cuddled into me and as she fell asleep. I stayed awake, playing with her hair for a while. Watching her for a little while longer, I made sure she was resting before I began answering any messages or emails I had ignored.

AFTER ABOUT A COUPLE OF HOURS, I left Kim to sleep and went downstairs to the kitchen to make some food. As much as I didn't want to leave her, I was practically wasting away, my stomach growling was sure to wake her. I tried to eat every day at the same time, but as I was enjoying myself too much with her in my arms, I skipped a meal.

Gratefully I found her fridge stocked to the brim with plenty to choose from. An omelet was however the easier choice. I tossed in some cooked ham, cheese and peppers as well as added some hot sauce I found in the cupboard. Once cooked, I sat down at the breakfast nook and watched the snow fall.

The house itself was beautiful. Nicely decorated, not over the top girly, but it was obvious a girl lived here. The house smelt of pine and her floral perfume. The entire house breathed Kimberly. Frames decorated the walls of champion figure skaters, her medals as well as photographs and news clippings from her competitions.

After I left town, I had tried my best to keep up with Kim's sporting journey. It was important that I knew she succeeded in what she wanted to do with her life. When the news broke she had married her boyfriend from university, I didn't read many things after that. I would only catch the odd sports interview then, she just stopped competing altogether.

Now I know the reason. She had to give up her dream and I wasn't sure if that was one hundred percent what she wanted to do. After I finished eating, I made sure to clean up after myself and at some point Daisy had joined me which meant, Kim may have been awake.

"Yes, mom, we will be round."

Her voice drifted down the stairs as she appeared in a pair of skinny fit jeans and a figure-hugging white t-shirt which left little to my imagination. She stopped in the kitchen doorway as she spotted me still in my gray sweatpants sipping at my coffee.

"Keep looking at me like that and we won't make it to my parents."

"Well, when you come downstairs looking like that, how can I not stare at you."

"Sam, we have places to be, things to do."

Coming up to the counter next to me, she poured herself a cup of coffee. I placed my cup down before coming up behind her and hugging her from behind, kissing lightly on her neck.

"Oi, what did I just say?" She declared, pouring the cream into her drink.

"Can't I kiss you?"

"You know what happens when you kiss me like that."

"I have no idea what you're talking about and besides, I'm not going to throw myself at you. A man like me needs to be wooed a little."

Nipping at her earlobe, I let go quickly and went to turn away. She quickly pulled me back, bringing my face down to hers and kissing me roughly on the lips. I didn't think she would have actually wanted to do anything judging from what happened earlier, but I was happy to roll with it.

"I guess, we can be a little late for dinner." She winked.

"Say no more."

Kissing her deeply then, I lifted her up onto the breakfast counter as she pushed away anything that was behind her. My hands were already on her t-shirt, pulling it up over her head as her hands explored my bare chest and then started to pull my sweatpants down off my hips.

"Someone's eager," she said as she released my erection. I growled against her lips as her hands wrapped around it.

"Look who's talking, can't keep your hands off me."

Pulling at her hair a little, I tugged her head back, exposing her neck. Using my free hand to undo the button on her jeans. Pushing her to lie down on the counter, I yanked the jeans off, turning them inside out as well as her red panties. I pulled her a little forward so I could begin kissing her up her thighs then on her center.

She moaned as my tongue flicked at her clit and I started to taste her. Her hands were already finding my hair as she pushed my head a little bit. My tongue diving deep within her wet core and I lapped her up, enjoying every movement, every sound she made. Her orgasm reached her and the sound that erupted from her mouth made me moan against her.

Hot, a little flushed, she pulled my head up a little, tugging at my hair and was already sitting up on her elbows. She looked so sexy, and I just wanted to bury myself deep within her again. Lifting her up to sit on my hips, I found her and moaned as I entered her. Allowing her to ride me as I held her up. Kissing her neck, jawline as she wrapped her arms around my head and moaned deeply, loudly.

God, this woman was going to be the death of me.

I would happily lose myself in her as we picked up the pace, finding the floor seconds later. Her back against the stoned floor as I picked up the speed and just as I was about to finish, I realized the one thing we were missing.

Shit.

Thinking fast as I reached my peak, I pulled out quickly and not only did I finish on my sweatpants but also all over Kim's stomach. To which we both looked at each other a little surprised then she laughed. Thank God she laughed as I thought she would yell at me.

"Okay, maybe I should leave condoms downstairs as well."

She joked, leaning up again to kiss me on the lips. She was quick to stand up, finding some kitchen towels to clean herself up and handing me some.

"You best clean yourself up, we have to be at my parents at ten."

CHAPTER 26
Kimberly

Nerves struck hard as we stepped onto the front porch of mom and dad's house. I had avoided the place all week, even yesterday I made Joe meet me at the bar. I had managed to get mom on the phone earlier to tell her Sam had arrived in town early and asked if it would it be alright if I brought him to dinner. She didn't seem all that impressed, but dad soon changed her mind and said it would be a great idea.

Linking his fingers in mine, I thought Sam looked handsome and dressed up a little more than the casual we originally planned. He must have tried on five shirts before he settled on a pair of dark blue jeans, a grey plaid shirt, his black timberlands, and a thick denim wool lined jacket.

"It will be fine; you know I will be on my best behavior and will take any brunt they throw at me."

"I know you will, I'm just worried mom can be quite nasty after a drink...and now I know of your past, I don't want her upsetting you."

"You're sweet, but I'm a big boy, I will be fine."

I hated knowing now what he must have gone through;

especially the trauma. I couldn't even imagine having a parent that took their anger out on me. My dad was a big softie, he always helped anyone he could, put himself last, was kind and my hero. My mom, although more of a pain in the ass as I got older, she was still my go to person for everything. She was my rock. And I knew she was just being protective.

"Are we going in then?"

Sam asked, lifting my knuckles up to brush against his lips. His green eyes sparkled against the porch Christmas lights. Dad took great pride in decorating for Christmas. His was usually the best house on the block. It was never over the top, but always a beautiful display of fairy lights, with Santa and his sleigh on the roof and a nativity display in the front yard.

Turning the handle of the front door, Daisy rushed in first, as she usually did. I heard mom in the kitchen shouting happily that her 'furgrandbaby' had arrived. Then she poked her head out the archway that led to the kitchen and gave me a little cheery wave.

"Be with you in a moment my love, just basting the chicken."

Sam gave my hand a reassuring squeeze as we turned into the living room. Bethan and Joe were squabbling over something written on a piece of paper, while dad sat on the couch watching football.

"Oh, who's playing?"

"The Tiger-Cats and Red-Blacks."

Sam let go of my hand and stood behind the couch to see the game, crossing his arms, and going full dad pose. Beth and Joe hadn't even noticed us coming in as Beth threw up her arms looking a little red in the face. Mom was pottering around in the kitchen. I wasn't too sure if I should go in and offer some help, break the ice as we hadn't seen each other in a few weeks. Both of us had actively been trying to avoid one another.

Deciding to see what was wrong with my brother first was the best bet. We were only two days away from the wedding and I couldn't have the bride and groom arguing. Joe looked still worse for wear, and I was sure I could still smell some liquor on his breath.

"What's the matter, you two?"

"Joe has now changed his mind over the song choices! And we must confirm by tonight." Beth shouted a little.

Usually, she was as quiet as a mouse, but the wedding had really brought out her inner diva. I liked it. It made her a little more interesting.

"Joe, what's wrong with the picks? You guys took weeks to decide, and you can't really change your mind now." I looked at him as he sheepishly looked away.

"I just think they're a bit silly. We have like a million songs in the world to choose from and she wants some stupid boy band as our first dance."

"They're not just some stupid boy band!! OD is my life!"

"See now you're just being overdramatic."

I felt my own anger rise up then. Beth wasn't being over-dramatic, she just loved her boy bands. Most girls did, I still had a soft spot for an all-boy American boy band from the 90s. I would happily listen to their music well until my old age.

Beth shoved from the table and stormed into the kitchen, which I didn't blame her for. She had done most of the leg work for this wedding. I helped as much as I could with the decorating and corresponding with the wedding planner for her, but for the most part it had just been Beth.

"Well, that was a dickhead move, Joe."

"I know, she's just been so pissy lately."

Holding his head in his hands, I wasn't sure if this was a

talk he needed from his big sister or his best man-lady. Taking one of his hands in mine, he looked at me with a gross face. Then he realized I wasn't going to let go even if he tried to pull away.

"Weddings are stressful. Remember how bad I was at mine, I panicked whenever anything went wrong or changed. But I will tell you something, I have no idea what my songs were. I can just remember walking down the aisle to meet Luke and our first dance. I just remember the happy feeling I felt all day, and how my face hurt when it ended as I spent the entire day smiling."

His eyes lowered again as I let go of his hand, wondering if he was taking my words in. I slightly remembered my first dance song with Luke, it was a James Blunt song that Luke absolutely loved and would play all the time.

"I should apologize."

"Yes, you should."

One thing about Joe that I always loved was he was always quick to admit when he was wrong. Well, at least with everyone else, his big sis not so much. I was always the one to blame when he did something wrong and got away with it. We had many arguments as teens because of it. It didn't help that we were so close in age either.

"Would you ever get married again?"

Sam took Joe's seat and I looked at him shocked at his sudden question.

"I'm not asking, don't worry! If I were to ever ask, it wouldn't be in your parents living room."

"Ha ha, umm – Maybe."

I had no idea why I became so flustered when he asked. The truth was, I hadn't even thought about sleeping with another person after Luke, so I was surprised to even do that. Maybe marriage again, one day, but not for many years.

"Dinners ready!"

Mom shouted from the kitchen and as always, dad was the last one to join us in the dining room.

"Sam, you're sitting next to me."

Mom commanded as she took her usual seat next to the head of the table, where dad sat. Sam was stuck in between her and Joe who sat at the other end. I didn't think of this situation, I thought Sam could sit next to me and mum would have asked Beth to sit next to her, like she normally does. Instead, Beth sat next to me and still looked angry.

"Beth, whatever happens on your wedding day is going to be perfect," I whispered to her as she took a sip of her wine.

She gave me a small smile in return, and we waited for mom to say grace. Although we weren't that religious, this was something we had always done since I could remember. Thankfully Sam went along with it.

"So, Samuel, are you officially back in town? Or are you just planning to visit again?"

Round one. Mom.

"For the moment, I will be here for a few days. After the wedding, I will be back and forth to the rink, finishing the training on the hockey team as well as overseeing the charity match preparations."

"I see. Will you eventually move back here? That is if you stay with Kim."

"That's for Kim to decide what she wants to do; I will go wherever she wants me to."

Point one to Sam as mom mmm'ed and cut into her chicken. Her eyes found me from across the table and they didn't seem at all warm or welcoming. Shooting a look then towards dad, he drank his glass of beer and cleared his throat. Obviously next up on the interrogation.

"Do you have any plans to retire then? Ice hockey isn't that big in our little town, which would only mean you'd be traveling a lot."

"Again, it would be up to Kim. I don't plan to retire anytime soon as long distance can work."

"Until it doesn't," Joe piped in, unexpectedly.

"Why is my relationship up for discussion at the dinner table anyways? Sam can do whatever he wants, as can I. If we want to be together, the least you guys could do is support us."

I didn't like how this conversation was going already. I just wanted to be happy. I hadn't been happy in a long time. Even when Luke was ill, I knew eventually I'd face his death and when it happened, it took my breath away and I felt my life fall apart. I've slowly been building it back up ever since and Sam just fell into it.

"We are just worried that you will get hurt again, Kimmy. He left you before and he will do it again."

"Mom, we were what seventeen? You can't judge Sam for something he did ten years ago. We've grown up since then, and we both moved on. And somehow we've managed to find each other again. This is all new and exciting and you don't know the truth of what happened that night."

"Kim, it's okay."

Sam looked at me from across the table, his face soft as I tried to keep some tears from escaping. I knew they were going to ask some questions. I knew they wanted to scold him for what he did to me at prom, but we had moved past it ourselves and moved on from it.

"The reason why I wasn't there for Kim, to collect her for prom... Which, can I assure you I have apologized for, and she has forgiven me. But, I didn't show up because I was embarrassed. I got into a fight with my father after he had a few too many drinks, like he did most weekends, and I ran. I didn't want to tell anyone as it had been going on for years. I just left and didn't ever look back."

They were all silent. Dad was the first one to defend him, which made sense. Dad knew Samuel's father since high school as they'd grown up together. I was pretty sure they still played golf once a month together. I hadn't mentioned it to Sam just in case it upset him. Which thinking about it now was wrong to keep from him.

"Karl? Don't be daft, he wouldn't hurt anyone. Let alone his kids."

"You don't always know what goes on behind closed doors." I replied.

Mom turned to look at Sam fully this time. I thought in that second, she might yell, shout, or do something, but instead she wrapped her arms around him. Which took all of us by surprise, including Sam.

"I am so sorry you had to grow up in a home that was like that."

Letting go of him, she looked at him with such kindness, it almost brought me to tears. I wasn't expecting my mother to be kind this evening, I thought she would continue with the cold shoulder towards Sam and me. I wanted to ask her why, why did she think that was okay and yet, here she was hugging him.

"Did he hit you? – You know, I always got a weird vibe from him."

"Anna, you can't be serious? Karl has been friends with us for many years!"

Dad pushed himself from the table and stood, looking at mom with anger. Mom stood her ground though. So much for a nice family dinner. Poor Beth looked a little weary as did Sam, whereas Joe continued to stuff his face, unbothered or unchanged by anything. Typical.

"I apologize, I didn't mean to cause an argument," Sam said over the sudden yelling.

"You don't need to apologize. If anything, we should be the ones to say sorry. For now, Noah and I are going to discuss this elsewhere, you guys just enjoy the food."

Taking hold of dad's hand, mom pulled him out towards the back porch and shut the door. They weren't the parents that argued in front of their kids. It was rare they did argue in front of us growing up and I guessed it was the same around house guests.

"Sorry, Kim, I didn't mean for that to happen."

"Don't sweat it," Joe said. "They will be fine as soon as they come back in. Bad luck in childhood though, bro. Explains why you were a bit of a dick in school."

Classic Joe held up his drink in a cheers motion and downed the rest of his water. He looked at Beth who rolled her eyes at him and excused herself from the table to which Joe followed straight after. Just leaving Sam and I alone.

The snow had gotten heavier while we were at Kim's parents' house. Once dinner had calmed down, we sat down in the living room. While the women seemed to be discussing the wedding, myself, Joe, and Noah sat and watched the rest of the football game.

Football was never really my thing, but he seemed to be trying to make amends or at least, to not discuss or ask questions about my parents. Both of which I still hadn't seen or bumped into. Occasionally I looked up over to Kim when I felt a pair of eyes watching me and she'd quickly look away.

The thought of my upbringing had clearly put a damper on the evening, and I wasn't sure how we were going to get past that. The weekend's event was going to be great fun and not awkward at all.

"Have you seen your parents since you've been back in town?" Noah asked out of the blue.

"Eh – No, I haven't. I know they know I'm here as it's pretty much front-page news."

"Do you plan on speaking to them?"

"Not if I can help it."

Noah huffed and turned back to watch the television. I knew I had to try and build that bridge again with Kim's dad. He was important to her and if I wanted to be permanent in her life, I would need her father to at least accept I was here to stay.

Realizing the air was going a little stale as I sat there, I opted to let Daisy out to do her business. I was hopeful Kim wanted to head back to hers soon. The night was coming in as was the snow the more hours we spent here. I trusted her driving, but driving in the snow was always a little difficult.

"So, about dad, he can be a bit touchy when his friends are brought up. Even if they are jerks."

I hadn't noticed Joe had followed me out. He puffed into one of those fancy vape machines and blew out a fruity smelling gas. I always thought they were a little stupid. If you were going to smoke, smoke a real cigarette at least.

"It's alright, understandable."

"Just a heads up though, your parents have been invited to the wedding."

Great. No wonder Noah asked if I would be seeing them. Kim hadn't mentioned it so either she didn't know, or she didn't think to say anything, maybe to ambush me? No, she wasn't like that. I didn't want to think she would hide something like that from me either.

"Just do me a favor, try not to cause a scene. It's a wedding after all."

Patting me on the back, I felt that old temper appearing inside me. If it wasn't for Daisy coming back and barking to go inside, I would have turned around and punched him in the face.

As I followed him back into the house, I just wanted to leave now. I wouldn't be the one causing a scene that was for sure. I was coming to the wedding for Kim's sake and only for

Kim. I would of course be on my best behavior. Paula would destroy me as well if I didn't do or say anything that wasn't up to PR standards.

"Kim, the snow is really coming down, are you almost ready to go?"

I hated to seem controlling, but the good mood I was in had disappeared. Now I just wanted to climb back into bed, fuck my girlfriend and go to sleep.

"Yeah, sure. We're good here."

Heading to get our coats, Kim hugged her mom tightly then hugged Beth. The women all seemed to be at ease, far more relaxed than they were earlier and I wish I could say the same.

"Beth, Joe, the wedding is going to be gorgeous and such a perfect day. I will see you bright and early Saturday morning, Joe."

Taking hold of my hand, she hooked Daisy onto her lead with the other. We said our goodbyes and headed out and as we did, the tightness in my chest loosened.

"SORRY ABOUT MY DAD EARLIER."

Kim sat on her vanity table, brushing her hair, or taking her earrings out, I wasn't sure. I had been semi staring into space since we came upstairs and started to prepare for bed. It was a little earlier than I was used to. But because the ride home had been colder than expected, she said cuddling in bed and sticking a film on would be nice.

I was happy to do whatever she wanted to do if I had her naked next to me. Instead, she had opted for a pair of pajamas with some rather fluffy socks with frogs dotted on them. She made me laugh as she came bouncing out of her bathroom. Happily she showed off her socks. I had been in a mood until she'd done that, but now, she was a little busy and I was left to let my mind wander.

"It's alright. But you didn't tell me my parents would be at the wedding."

She lowered her eyes from the mirror and turned half round to look at me, her brush still in her hand. First she looked sad then a little annoyed.

"I didn't think they were coming; they hadn't returned the rsvp as far as I was told. I would have said something if I had known."

I didn't want to start an argument with her, but I could feel one brewing. If she didn't know then that was fine, but she did know they'd been invited and hadn't said a word. Especially after what I told her, in confidence.

"Kim, you knew they were invited though and didn't say anything about it. So, it's either you didn't know, or you did know."

My voice was a little harsher than I wanted it to be. I couldn't punch her brother square in the face, and I had pushed that annoyance deep down. I wanted to yell just a little bit, even when it wasn't even her fault.

"I knew about their invitation, yes, but I didn't know they accepted. I wasn't entirely sure how I was meant to tell my brother about your business. That was for you to decide. If my parents and brother now contact your parents and de-invite them, that's up to them. Either way, the day will go ahead, and it will be wonderful," she paused, turning away from me again to face her mirror.

"One way or another you will have to face them. Every therapist would say the same thing as well. You can't hide from your problems or bury your head in the sand, and I should know."

Getting up without a word, I headed out the bedroom and went downstairs. I needed to cool off. I didn't want to lose my shit. I knew she was right, annoyingly. She knew more than anyone it wasn't good to run away from your feelings. Just earlier that day, I had witnessed her having to go through one of her own battles.

I sat downstairs for a while before she eventually came to join me and sat next to me on the couch. She wore some raggedy old looking cardigan that had a few holes in the sleeve, and she wrapped it around herself a little tightly.

"I don't wanna fight with you," she broke the silence, "I also didn't want to piss you off."

"You didn't piss me off. It was your brother, but don't worry about it. I shouldn't have snapped, I'm sorry."

"What did Joe do? Or say?"

"Doesn't matter, he's allowed to want his wedding to go smoothly. I won't be speaking to my parents. Unless of course, they speak to me and when they do, can you be at my side?"

Looking at her, she stared at me with tenderness in her eyes and placed a hand on my leg. I placed my hand over hers and squeezed a little.

"I will be at your side for as long as you want me to be. I am here to stay."

She didn't have to say any more than that, I knew what it meant. Picking her up to sit on my lap, I carried her up the set of stairs and headed towards her bedroom, where we didn't 'fuck'. But in the words of a romance novel, we made love, and it was sweet.

CHAPTER 28

Kimberly

The morning of the wedding arrived after a blissful Friday spent with Sam. We did have a lot of running around to do. We decorated mom and dad's back yard, prepped the wedding planner, got with the decorating team, kept Beth chilled and Joe from drinking himself silly.

Joe had opted to get ready at my house as Beth wanted mom and dad's as it was bigger and would fit all her girl-friends in. Thankfully dad stayed there as well, it meant there were no awkward conversations going on between him and Sam.

"Are you nervous about today?"

I asked Sam as I did up his red tie, which matched his gorgeous black velvet tuxedo. I was glad he opted for the black, rather than the red as that would have been very out there.

"Not as much as I thought I'd be. Today will go smoothly, your parents' house looks incredible. I think if you stop being a skating coach, wedding planning will be your fall back."

"I do enjoy it, but skating is my life."

"Don't I know it."

Kissing him softly on the lips before I turned around, he zipped up my dress. Catching the reflection of us both in the mirror, I felt a sudden rush of blood in my cheeks as he ran his hands down my forearms and kissed me lightly on the neck.

"My girlfriend is hot."

I was still getting used to him calling me his girlfriend. I wasn't as shocked as I was the first time he said it. It was over the phone with Jason yesterday afternoon. Although this whole thing started as fake dating, or a lie to cover our tracks, it hadn't ended that way.

"And dare I say, you will have all the ladies staring at you."

As he let go of me, I headed towards the guest bedroom where Joe was standing with one of his groomsmen, both getting in those much-needed photographs from the photographer. Posing as his cufflinks were done up and then I came in to fix his tie, which clearly no man was able to tie correctly.

"You ready?"

"I was born ready to marry Beth."

"Glad to hear it, we need to head over shortly."

He looked a little nervous when I mentioned the time as the photographer turned us around to get a photograph together. I didn't have the option for a buttonhole so instead Joe had gifted me a corsage of a white rose with red ribbon. It matched perfectly with the theme.

Neither him nor Bethan had seen the garden once we had finished decorating it. I was looking forward to seeing everyone's faces when they arrived.

With it being winter, the sun set a little earlier in the day so we had brought the ceremony forward as a special request from the photographer, so she could get those bride and groom photographs. It also meant Beth would get her first dance under the trail of fairy lights we had set up all around the garden and across the trees.

Dad had taken great pride in handling all the lights as well as dressing up the large oak tree. We had grown up playing in that tree in the backyard. My phone buzzed as the alarm I set went off to get everyone downstairs, to grab those group photos on my front porch which had also been decorated with lights around the beams, to keep with the theme.

"Right, time for photos downstairs then we will head over."

"Is my ring bearer ready to do her job?"

Joe asked as he kneeled down towards Daisy who had been sitting and waiting patiently at the bottom of the stairs. Wrapped around her neck was a beautiful red velvet ribbon and when the time was right, one of Joe's groomsmen was to tie on the wedding rings so she could head down towards him and Beth and give them their rings.

"I think she's the only one who's been ready for hours,"

Sam said as he leant against the doorframe.

Joe just smiled a little at him as he got up and did as he was told, heading downstairs with the rest of his team.

"He will come around, eventually."

Wrapping my arms around Sam's waist, he kissed me on the top of my head and hugged me tightly.

"I know, I'd be the same as him if my sister was dating my high school bully."

"Come on, we best get going otherwise we will be late ourselves."

BETH HAD ASKED, well demanded, that they could get a horse drawn carriage for some of their wedding photographs.

Which one of the local farmers were happy to offer, in exchange for photographs and a slice of cake.

It was one of the few things I loved about living in a small town, everyone helped each other when we could. Crystal had done all the catering along with the girls. They were sitting in the guest seating area when we all arrived.

And as the music started to play, we each took our places in the line to head down to the front. Sam thankfully sat with Crystal and the girls as they left him a seat, most likely desperate to ask for all the gossip.

Linking arms with Joe, we headed down after his groomsmen and no sooner than a few minutes later did Bethan and her bridesmaids arrive.

The photographer continued to snap away picture after picture, timed wonderfully as Joe dabbed his wet eyes once he spotted Bethan walking down our little garden aisle. Her eyes lit up as she looked around, spotting all the beautiful led glass lanterns we had set up. The fairy lights glittering in the snow lit sky as the snow fell slowly and lightly.

It was a perfect moment and she looked breathtaking in a fur shrug over her satin fitted mermaid dress. Something I myself had forgotten about as goosebumps trailed up my arms. I was normally used to the cold, but now I craved Sam's warm arms around me.

As they said their I do's, I held back the tears as my baby brother married the love of his life. Each time I looked over at Sam he too was smiling brightly at me. Perhaps this would be us one day. Maybe.

I was grateful once the ceremony and group photographs were over as my feet ached from the black Jimmy Choo pumps. I hadn't had a chance to break in yet and knew full well there were going to be a few blisters in the morning.

"Looks like you could use this."

Megan appeared holding out a glass of red wine and I took it without a second thought. Yes, I was parched and needed a good drink or three. Sam had been pulled to the dance floor by Crystal demanding he'd show her his shake your booty dance while Lacy enjoyed herself and danced with Jasmine.

"Are you happy with our meddling now?"

"You know as well as I do, I have never enjoyed any of you meddling in my life – but, this time round, I will say thank you."

"Good cause that's one fine piece of ass you are not allowed to lose. We all agree, he's good for you."

As the music began to slow into a slow dance, Taylor Swift started to blare out of the speakers and Sam instantly looked for me. Grabbing me seconds later, he pulled me into a soft waltz.

Throwing one of my arms around his neck, he swayed me, spun me out and then back into him. It felt as if everyone stopped to watch us. Thankfully it was just the girls as Megan held up her phone to capture a few pictures.

"I've loved you three summers..." Sam whispered in my ear, copying with the song and my heart melted a little.

"I think you will find you've loved me longer," I whispered back.

"I never stopped."

The evening was picture-perfect. Even to the point Sam's parents had barely said anything other than a few hellos and how are you. Which was sad, but I think they realized today wasn't the time and place. Eventually, Sam would speak to them, in his own time.

"I mean it, Kim. It has always been you, since the first day I met you, when you got stuck with me."

His voice sent shivers down my spine as he began to

confess his feelings and I rested my head against his chest as we rocked.

"I know you loved Luke, and you might still be in love with him, I understand that. But."

He lifted my chin up to face him, his eyes glassy and just as beautiful as they've always been. Green with specks of brown in them.

"I intend to be your last love. If you will have me."

I smiled as soon as he said the words. I knew in my heart what I wanted. He was my first love. Luke was my great love, but this...Sam would be my last love and one I was meant to be with for the rest of my life with.

"I love you, too."

His smile widened as he pulled me even closer to him, his lips finding mine and then he lifted me up a little. My leg bent at the knee and rose behind me, then he lowered me down again.

"We can't take all the spotlight," I said as his lips left mine.

A small laugh was shared between us. Thankfully no one was paying any attention to us as Bethan and Joe began cutting the cake. We had that moment to ourselves and although the music had been turned down, we continued to dance together.

We would dance together forever.

Acknowledgments

When I first really started getting into writing stories, I always wanted to write a contemporary romance. Instead, I went on to write a fantasy series and a paranormal romance series, clearly neither of which were just a contemporary romance.

I have always loved those meet cute love stories growing up. I watched The Notebook gosh know's how many times and I always enjoyed the happy ever after endings in a love story.

Funny how the books I've have written so far have always ended in some form of angst and cliff hangers. Writing Kim and Sam's story was as if I were a passenger in their cars and I just documented their stories.

I wanted to write something that felt real, something that may have happened to a couple in real life. Kimberly's story was inspired by so many I have heard throughout my life. And Sam's, we all knew a Sam in school growing up and I always wondered if they ended up happy.

I want to just give a small thank you to my PA Lisa, my beta readers who have been with me through the start of Kim & Sam's journey. Tayla, Charlene, Jess, Kayleigh and Kendrah. Thank you guys!

Of course, my husband Jack who had to put up with my giggling as I wrote those spicy scenes. Thank's for the inspiration ;)

And as always, thank you to you, my readers for allowing me to continue on this author, writing journey. I value each and every single one of you.

About the Author

Melanie Davies began writing when she was in her early teens, starting off first in vampire role play forums, she began to learn her voice and teach herself how to write creatively.

This is her fifth published book and she looks forward to bringing more fictional worlds and characters to you.

Writing has always been a dream of hers and one she is excited to achieve.

Also by Melanie Davies

A DANCE OF TWILIGHT

A fae filled magical world, following the story of Ornella and her Shadow Man. This is the first book in this World Series.

Each book will follow a different couple and can be

read on own.

A Dance Of Twilight

THE MIDNIGHT STAKES SERIES

A paranormal romance inspired by Van Helsing and Buffy the vampire slayer. Filled with found family, spice, a badass female lead and a mysterious male lead.

Graveyard Shift | Taken To The Grave

NIMRA WORLD SERIES

A fantasy romance full of unforgettable twists & turns, found family, a strong female lead, and a morally grey mc. Slow burn to spice, multi-pod.

The Sapphire Oath - The Emerald Truth

Made in United States
Orlando, FL
16 December 2024

55814658R00131